## "Fran, Do You Trust Me?"

The softly spoken question took her aback with its unexpectedness.

"Why, yes, I suppose so," she said finally.

He turned her around to face him, and she could see the humorous slant of his mouth.

"If you trust me, you have to believe I wouldn't ask you to do anything beyond your capabilities or detrimental to your well-being."

"I guess I can try," she murmured uncertainly. How could she hope to resist his will when he stood so close that his masculinity was a tangible force assaulting her senses, holding her captive?

---

CAROLE HALSTON
is the wife of a sea captain, and writes while her husband is out at sea. Her characters frequently share her own love of nature and enjoyment of active outdoor sports.

Dear Reader:

I'd like to take this opportunity to thank you for all your support and encouragement of Silhouette Romances.

Many of you write in regularly, telling us what you like best about Silhouette, which authors are your favorites. This is a tremendous help to us as we strive to publish the best contemporary romances possible.

All the romances from Silhouette Books are for you, so enjoy this book and the many stories to come. I hope you'll continue to share your thoughts with us, and invite you to write to us at the address below:

Karen Solem
Editor-in-Chief
Silhouette Books
P.O. Box 769
New York, N.Y. 10019

# CAROLE HALSTON
## Sunset in Paradise

*Silhouette Romance*
Published by Silhouette Books New York
**America's Publisher of Contemporary Romance**

**Other Silhouette Books by Carole Halston**

*Stand-in Bride*
*Love Legacy*
*Keys to Daniel's House*
*Undercover Girl*
*Collision Course*

SILHOUETTE BOOKS, a Simon & Schuster Division of
GULF & WESTERN CORPORATION
1230 Avenue of the Americas, New York, N.Y. 10020

ISBN: 0-671-57208-3

First Silhouette Books printing March, 1983

10 9 8 7 6 5 4 3 2 1

# Sunset in Paradise

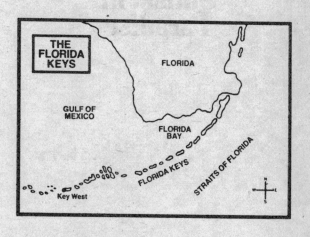

# Chapter One

*Quite a crowd at Sunset this afternoon,* Fran noted, shrugging aside her despondency as she parked her bicycle before mounting the steps to the broad pier. Sunburned tourists formed little knots around the entertainers stationed at intervals along the two-hundred-odd feet of sturdy concrete barrier between historic Mallory Square and the Gulf of Mexico.

The juggling act was going a little better than it had that afternoon on the beach. When one of the new guys fouled up, the old-timers George and Bimbo would really clown it up, to the wholehearted delight of the audience. With a frankly assessing gaze, Fran surveyed the smiling faces of the tourists as if gauging their generosity by the rapt expressions. With any luck, they would show their appreciation with money, which was badly needed by the impromptu performers to supplement meager incomes from low-paying jobs, if they were lucky enough to have jobs at all.

It seemed grossly unfair to Fran that a paradise like Key West was barely affordable for those who could most enjoy its tropical allure: the young people who had not yet taken upon their shoulders those burdens imposed by maturity, responsibilities of career, marriage and family. Year after year they continued to flock to the southernmost tip of the continental United States, drawn by the magic of clear turquoise water and white sand beaches bathed in the brilliance and warmth of the tropical sun. Somehow they managed to support themselves, for a few weeks or months or perhaps even a year, before they returned to less idyllic surroundings to resume college studies or embark upon a career.

Until just recently Fran had considered herself one of the lucky people in the world, those who lived year-round in Key West. But now that Aunt Liz was moving back to Georgia, and selling the house, Fran faced the appalling possibility that she might not be able to afford to stay here, not on her minimum-wage salary from the Lemon Tree Boutique.

Resolutely shoving aside that unsettling prospect and the aching unhappiness it invariably caused her, Fran moved along to the next group of watchers, surmising from their large number and high degree of animation that the performer in their midst must be Mike the Magician. All those newcomers to Key West aspiring to entertain at Sunset could take a lesson from him. He set about immediately developing a laughing rapport with his audience, and his act was timed perfectly so that his charming request for money came just before everyone's attention turned to the grand event of the afternoon, the huge red sun's descent into the ocean.

Fran strolled along enjoying the familiar scene. Far out to the horizon stretched the darkening sea, ruffled by a cool evening breeze. The sun was a molten ball of red-orange suspended in a flamboyant sky shading from cerise to palest lavender. Shrimp boats glided past on their way into harbor, their draped black nets resembling the huge webbed wings of an insect. At closer range, a large yacht under full sail swished by only daring yards from the concrete pier, the party lounging in the cockpit, sipping drinks, the object of much good-natured envy from those on shore.

Everywhere Fran looked were expensive-looking cameras trained this way and that, being endlessly adjusted in the compulsive effort to capture the essence of the moment on film. In a way she pitied them—the tourists. They were in Key West for a few carefree days and then had to return to wherever they had come from. She, on the other hand, would live on this island forever, her very heartbeat in tune with the hauntingly beautiful, ever elusive spirit that was Key West. For somehow she *would* manage to stay, even if it meant working so many jobs she had almost no leisure time.

*"Hey, Fran!"*

An underlying note of pleading in the salutation arrested her attention, bringing her out of the reverie. She had reached the farthest end of the pier in the direction of Duval Street, where a half dozen youths were endeavoring to play an incongruous variety of musical instruments. Judging from their own embarrassed manner and the sparse gathering of listeners, they were enjoying limited success in their first venture to entertain the crowds at Sunset. Every one of them a newcomer to Key West, they hadn't much time for practice together. A desperate shortage of funds had given them impetus to brave the Sunset audience before they were confident.

Without a second's hesitation, Fran responded to the implicit cry for help. Joining the flustered group, she spoke a few smiling instructions and began singing a simple folk ballad that they would have no trouble accompanying. Before her clear melodic voice had sounded the final plaintive repetition of the refrain, the crowd had grown as if by magic.

With the instincts of the natural performer, she smiled and spoke to her audience in a conversational tone that made each person feel she was speaking personally just to him. Before she could lose anyone's attention, she launched into a popular country-rock number with a livelier tempo, moving with lithe rhythm to the infectious beat.

Then, to the utter delight of her audience, she moved from one musician to the next playing a few notes on each of the instruments—violin, accordion, guitars, and last, the hammer dulcimer, a silvery-toned instrument resembling a small table on legs. Coming to the end of the song with a showy flourish of notes, she thanked the enthusiastically applauding audience for their kindness.

Judging the time to be about right—the sun would be eclipsing their act in about ten minutes—she plucked the worn black beret from the head of the lanky accordion player, a kid from Denver named Arthur, and held it out in a charmingly suppliant gesture. "Bless you," she murmured, passing along the inside of the circle as crisp bills and handfuls of coins dropped into the beret.

Completely lacking self-consciousness, she moved with natural grace among the crowd, tall and slender in a full, gathered skirt and low-scooped peasant blouse in colors as exotic as the foliage of the island. Her long, honey-brown hair, streaked with gold, hung in two heavy braids. Her skin was a deep golden brown from hours on the beach every day. Her mouth, full and sensitive, hinted at every subtle change of mood. Most remarkable of her features, though, were the eyes. Fringed with long, gold-tipped lashes, they were the same startling blue as the crystalline water surrounding Key West.

Emanating youth, superb good health and a natural beauty, she moved among the crowd accepting their offerings, noticing with satisfaction the growing pile of paper bills among the coins. The guys in the band would be able to eat tonight.

It came as an abrupt shock to look up into the face of a tall man and see the aloofness in his wintry gray eyes. For one long breathless instant, she gazed up into the sternly handsome features, reading there the shrewd appraisal of her artless manipulation of the crowd. At once angry with herself for feeling so nakedly vulnerable under his piercing gaze, and resentful of him for having the power to so disconcert her, she flashed him a dazzling smile and made a graceful little gesture to draw his attention to the beret.

Not taking his eyes from her face, he reached for his wallet and very deliberately extracted a crisp paper bill, folded it lengthwise in lean, strong fingers and tucked it into the neckline of her blouse. She gasped and recoiled from the touch of his flesh, angry color flooding her face and neck. Plucking the bill from between her breasts, she saw with incredulity that it was a twenty-dollar bill!

"Thank you, Mister," she murmured and edged past him, aware for the first time of the sleek blonde woman standing next to him. She was noticeable in the casually attired crowd for the expensive elegance of her clothing and the utterly bored expression on her face. Cool blue eyes mirrored distaste as they surveyed Fran, making her feel absurdly young and unsophisticated in her brightly-hued skirt and blouse and brown leather sandals.

From the possessive manner in which the woman clung to the tall man's arm, she must be his wife. No doubt she was annoyed at the large denomination of her husband's contribution, not to mention his unconventional manner of bestowing it.

All pleasure in the cajoling of money from the onlookers had suddenly dissipated. Fran returned to the center of the crowd once more and with a theatrical gesture emptied the contents of the beret into one of the instrument cases lying open on the ground. Then she extended both arms toward the western horizon where the sun was a molten sphere resting on the rim of the ocean. As everyone watched, spellbound, it slid quickly into the ocean, leaving behind a ruddy glow.

Spontaneous applause erupted along the length of the pier. Sunset was over for today. As if released from a spell, tourists milled about, talking and laughing and making plans for the evening ahead. The denim-clad young entertainers busied themselves packing up the instruments and other paraphernalia employed in their acts.

Fran quickly forgot the tall, imposing stranger as she joined into the spirited banter of a group of some fifteen or twenty of her friends. Their good-natured jibes and unaffected laughter warmed her soul through and through, making her feel liked and accepted for herself. It had to be the greatest feeling in the world to be young and carefree among kindred spirits in this tropical paradise.

"Let's go get something to eat!" somebody sang out, and the suggestion met with overwhelming enthusiasm. By unspoken agreement they bypassed the high-priced tourist places and trooped along narrow back streets to a small Cuban café whose outside, painted a garish pink, wasn't impressive, but which offered good food reasonably priced.

Their arrival was greeted with welcome by the owners, two brothers who looked identical and ran the restaurant with the help of their wives and children. In spite of the young people's high-spirited banter and laughter, they were all basically well-behaved, never causing problems and seldom deserving the criticisms leveled by some of the local merchants who frowned upon any but the wealthy visiting their island.

Fran sat at a booth with several of the boys who rented rooms from her Aunt Liz. Two of them, Hank and Kevin, were members of the musical group she had rescued from utter failure at Sunset, and now they launched into a recounting of the brief episode for those who hadn't witnessed her performance.

There wasn't a lull in the conversation until the food was served. Fran eyed her barbecue-on-bun without any appetite, a condition not at all common for her. Underneath the air of celebration, the optimism that life was good, lurked a shadowy threat which spoiled her enjoyment of the company of her friends. Where would she and the dozen boys who rented rooms in Aunt Liz's rambling old house live once it was sold? Not only was it expensive to rent living quarters in Key West, where the smallness of the island caused land to sell for exorbitant prices, but every boarding house and apartment building had a long waiting list.

"Fran, you were really good!" Kevin broke into her gloomy introspection. "You ought to be singing in a band and making some real money instead of working for peanuts in that little dress shop."

"I've had offers," Fran admitted. "Aunt Liz doesn't think a night club is a healthy working atmosphere for a girl—" She heard the evasive note in her voice and knew from the curious expression in Kevin's eyes that he wasn't entirely satisfied with her explanation. While it was true Aunt Liz had objected to her performing in night clubs, that had been several years ago. Fran was almost twenty now and old enough to make her own decisions. The truth was there were other reasons, reasons too repugnant to bring out and examine, let alone discuss, that made her avoid pursuing a singing career that would put her up on a lighted stage before rowdy nightclub audiences.

Feeling herself the object of attention from the table next to the booth in which she sat, Fran glanced over and saw that Bob Silver had overheard the exchange and was regarding her with a thoughtful expression. "Kevin's right, you know. You should be singing with a band. Ginger's leaving in a couple of weeks. Why don't you think about taking her place?"

"That's a shame you're losing Ginger," Fran said quickly. "It won't be easy to get somebody with her kind of voice."

Bob's eyes slid over Fran, lingering an extra second on the shapely curves under her loose peasant blouse. "There's a lot more than singing involved in being a good female vocalist. Think about it, Fran. You've got what it takes."

The blatant assessment in Bob's gaze disturbed Fran more than it should have considering her age and extraordinary loveliness. In that measuring glance he had forcibly reminded her of what she would have to contend with if she agreed to become the vocalist for his musical group, who called themselves the Silver-Stringed Vagrants and currently were one of the most popular bands in Key West. At the present time they were playing an engagement at the Black Pig, a boisterous night spot on Duval Street.

"I'll think about it," she told Bob and transferred her attention back to those at her own table, who had been taking in the conversation between her and Bob with great interest. They might have pursued it if another subject of more immediate concern to all of them hadn't arisen.

"Too bad, Mrs. Todd has to find a buyer for the house," Hank said thoughtfully.

Detecting the underlying note of worry, Fran felt a rush of sympathy that exacerbated her own frustration and helplessness. *Why* did things have to change this way? *Why* did Aunt Liz have to sell the house and move back to Georgia, leaving Fran and a dozen young male boarders homeless? *Why?*

She knew the answer and so did Hank and Kevin and the others. There was no need for her to repeat it all again, but she couldn't seem to help herself.

"She can't afford to keep up the house any more. It needs a new roof. Do you have any *idea* what a new roof costs? The paint is peeling off. The plumbing all needs to be redone—" Fran broke off, regretting the strident edge of her voice when she saw the expressions on the faces of the boys and realized what they were thinking: if all Liz Todd's boarders were conscientious about paying their rent and if she charged them the going rate, she wouldn't have such trouble making ends meet.

Fran's voice was gentler as she continued. "Aunt Liz says Key West has changed so much she doesn't feel at home here anymore. It's gotten too crowded and commercial. She wants to go back to the place where she grew up. And now that her sister's husband is dead and Mrs. Edna wants Aunt Liz to come and live with her, it seems the perfect solution to her problems. With the money from the house, she'll be able to live comfortably until she's old enough to collect social security as Uncle John's widow."

The boys already knew that Aunt Liz's husband had died twelve years ago of a heart attack, but she had been ineligible to collect a widow's benefits until she was sixty-two. In the interim she had managed to subsist by taking in young male boarders, more often than not acting as surrogate mother as well as landlady.

"Mrs. Todd's not really your blood kin, is she?" Hank asked hesitantly.

"No, her husband, my Uncle John, was my father's brother." Fran's tone invited no further exploration of her past. After all these years, the word *father* still had a bitter taste and stuck in her throat.

It dawned on her suddenly what Hank and the other boys must be thinking, that because Aunt Liz was Fran's aunt only by marriage, Aunt Liz was abandoning her. Fran hastened to correct that misconception.

"Aunt Liz wants me to go back to Georgia, too. But it happens to be the last place I'd ever want to live." The idea of returning to the surroundings where she'd known nothing but unhappiness brought an irrepressible shudder, but she dragged her thoughts away from the quagmire of the past. That was all dead now and she didn't intend to let the memory of her father taint the present. He'd lost his hold over her when he died seven years ago. Since then she'd proved him *wrong,* wrong about herself and probably wrong about her mother, too.

"Hank, I heard the Ramada Inn is looking for waiters." With that brisk remark, she effectively changed the course of the conversation, and nothing more was said about the imminent possibility that in a few weeks time, none of them sitting together at the booth would have a roof over their heads.

When the gathering broke up a half hour later, Fran declined several invitations to join various groups in their plans for the evening. It was still early, but she was in no mood to be good company.

The old house on Whitehead Street looked gracious and dignified in the moonlight, which kindly concealed the signs of age and deterioration. Fran paused on the sidewalk outside the white picket fence looking up at its facade, reflecting with sadness that soon it would no longer be her home and haven as it had been for seven wonderful years. The wide planks of the porch seemed to groan tiredly under her feet as she walked across them, the sound somehow reminding her she was being very selfish giving in to her feelings like this. Aunt Liz felt bad enough as it was. Fran would be acting the ingrate to make her feel any worse. After all, this old house had been Aunt Liz's home for many more years than it had been Fran's, and it was not the older woman's fault that circumstances conspired to make selling it an economic necessity.

Straightening her shoulders and summoning an expression she meant to be cheerful, Fran entered the front hallway and made her way to the rear apartment which she shared with her aunt.

"Aunt Liz, I'm home," she called out as she entered the living room.

"Fran?" Worry etched lines in Liz Todd's weathered face as she swept into the room wearing a voluminous caftan of brightly printed cotton. Tendrils of brilliant orange hair escaped the untidy bun on top of her head and frizzed around her face. Fran wondered with wry amusement how Aunt Liz was going to adjust to life in a small rural Georgia town after years in the casual atmosphere of Key West, where eccentricities were easily tolerated.

"Anything wrong, Aunt Liz?"

*"Everything's* wrong, love." The older woman pressed the palms of both hands against her forehead in a distraught gesture. "Edna called about an hour ago. She fell off a ladder and broke her hip—can you imagine a woman her age climbing a ladder? Trying to fire a wasp nest, she said. It's a wonder she didn't burn down the whole house. Then not five minutes after she called, Joan Ellis was on the phone telling me she had the house sold—to some fellow from Maine, of all places! And Edna wants me to come to Georgia right away. She can't do a thing with this broken hip—oh, it's all too much in one night!"

Fran felt weak in the knees and would have liked to drop into one of the overstuffed chairs whose frayed upholstery was concealed by bright chintz slipcovers. Instead she walked over to her aunt and hugged her gently before steering her to the sofa. She couldn't agree with Aunt Liz more—it all *was* too much—but it was up to her to reassure her aunt.

"It's too bad about Mrs. Edna, but I guess it could have been worse, couldn't it?" she soothed. "And now that the house is sold, you can go to Georgia and leave all the paper work to Mrs. Ellis." Underneath her calm manner Fran was thinking, *Oh, no, it's all really happening. Aunt Liz is moving away. The house is being sold to a stranger. Where will I live? How can I make enough money to support myself?*

"But Fran, love, what about *you?*" Aunt Liz wailed.

"Me? I'll be fine, Aunt Liz, I promise you."

"Won't you come with me to Georgia? You don't make enough money at that dress shop to support yourself. . . . Honey, it's so *expensive* to live here."

It wasn't easy to resist her aunt's pleading tone or the love and concern mirrored in her features. Fran searched desperately for something to offer as proof she could take care of herself.

"I have an offer of a new job that not only will pay a lot more money—it may even make me a local celebrity. Now, Aunt Liz, don't look like that! I'm twenty years old. I can take care of myself!" The tone of indignation was more self-defense than anything else. Fran wished she herself felt better about taking the job Bob Silver had offered her with his band.

"Fran, you know how I feel about you singing in a night club."

"I do know, Aunt Liz, and I'm sorry to cause you any worry. But I'm a big girl now. So what about this old codger from Maine who's buying the house?"

Fran could tell by her aunt's expression that she was not happy about dropping the subject of Fran's future, but after a few seconds, she grudgingly answered.

"I don't know how old he is, but he can't be too young, judging from the money he must have. Joan says this house is only one of five he's buying—"

"Why does he need *five* houses?" Fran interrupted incredulously.

"He's planning to renovate them for resale."

Something exploded inside Fran and the bitterness boiled out before she could stop its molten flow. "You mean, he isn't even going to *live* in this house? It's not fair, Aunt Liz! Just because he has a lot of money!"

# Chapter Two

A heavy pall hung over the section of Smathers Beach that Fran and her friends frequented. In place of the usually energetic volleyball game, several deeply bronzed young males batted the ball back and forth in a desultory fashion. A trio of despondent youths went through the motions of rehearsing a mime act for Sunset later in the afternoon, but there was no heart in it.

Fran lay on her stomach with her chin resting on her forearm, staring sightlessly out to sea. Aunt Liz had departed yesterday morning for Georgia, following much insistence on Fran's part that she would be perfectly all right staying in the apartment until she had to move out.

"Aunt Liz, you *know* you can trust me," Fran had assured.

"I know, love," Aunt Liz had soothed, "but it doesn't really *look* right, you staying in a house with all boys." She had given in because she did trust her niece, fully aware that Fran was like a sister to the boys living in the house. More than once Liz Todd had worried that Fran wasn't more "normal," never going out on real dates but preferring to move about in groups where she wasn't paired off with one young man.

"Remember, love, if you can't find a nice place you can afford, you can always come and live with me and Edna," Aunt Liz reminded, right up to the last minute.

"I know," Fran replied, controlling only with an effort the ripple of revulsion that threatened at the thought of returning to the town in Georgia where she had lived with her father in a small gloomy house whose very bricks might have been mortared with his pessimism about life and bitterness against women, her mother in particular.

For several years before he died, her strongest wish had been someday to prove him wrong about the mother she had never known. She vowed that when she grew up, she would hire investigators to trace her mother and learn the truth behind her abandonment of husband, child and home. That determination had faded under the benign healing powers of the Key West sun during the last seven years, and Fran's most pressing concern at the moment was not to delve into the past and vindicate her mother's actions, but to manage somehow to continue living on this small island where she had learned self-worth and peace of mind. Key West was the soil that had nurtured her beleaguered soul: to leave it would be tantamount to ripping out a delicate plant by the roots.

"It's just not fair!" Fran raged, sitting up abruptly and drawing startled glances from those around her. The volleyball rested under the brawny arm of one of the disconsolate players. The halfhearted rehearsal of the mime act ceased altogether. Those lying on the sand nearby either sat up or turned so that they faced Fran, who became even more incensed at the apathy and resignation in their expressions and listless posture.

"He has no *right* to throw us out of our homes!" Her shrill tone grated on her own ears. She sounded as if she were trying to convince them of the injustice she perceived in the actions of the real estate developer from Maine, a Mr. Jonathan Talbot, who was purchasing five of the run-down old Conch houses on Whitehead Street with plans to restore them to their former elegance.

Two of the houses were currently in use as boarding houses, while one was divided into six apartments, the tenants of all three houses being young people about Fran's age. Altogether, more than thirty people had been given notice by Mrs. Ellis, the real estate agent acting for Mr. Talbot, to be off the premises no later than thirty days from the time of notice, which had been yesterday afternoon. On top of Aunt Liz's departure, it had been another devastating blow for Fran.

"He bought the houses, Fran."

"Yeah, man, he's the owner now."

"What can anybody *do?*"

Fran listened to the half-apologetic comments, hearing with dull misery the undertone of defeat. They weren't even willing to *try* to do anything, she reflected bitterly. More than thirty people were being bulldozed out of their homes and they weren't even going to make an effort to stand up for their human rights.

"Maybe if somebody *talked* to him, explained the situation—maybe he'd at least give us some more time," she pleaded, glancing around from face to face and seeing nothing but embarrassment and evasiveness. "Okay," she blazed, "*I'll* do it. If he's still here, I'll go and talk to him myself."

"Atta girl, Fran!"

"Can't hurt to try!"

Mixed in with the admiration for her spunk and the sheepishness for their own defeatism, Fran saw unspoken curiosity in her friends' faces. Some of them were wondering why she was so upset over this development: even if her pay at the dress shop was small, a pretty girl like herself wouldn't have any trouble finding a place to stay. Any number of guys on the island would be happy to share their living quarters with her. But that type of arrangement was definitely out of the question for Fran.

Too restless to relax now that she had taken upon herself the daunting task of speaking in person to the wealthy man who was becoming the owner of Aunt Liz's house and four others in its proximity, Fran left the beach. Pedaling her ten-speed along narrow residential streets, she surrendered her senses to the familiar beauty all around her. Huge crotons flaunted leaves heavily veined in crimson and yellow; bougainvillea climbed walls and sprawled along picket fences, displaying glorious masses of purple and magenta blossoms; the delicate greenery of hibiscus shrubs bore exquisite trumpets of pink, red and white. Overhead, the sky arced a clear and limitless blue, and the sunshine encompassed her with its brilliant warmth. This kind of weather in January!

How she loved all this, the tropical lushness, the languorous way of life, and most of all, the *freedom*. Freedom to be herself, to feel good about who she was and what she was, contrary to all her father's dire exhortations about the wicked nature of the female and the wanton characteristics Fran was sure to develop like all of her sex.

So lost was she in introspection, Fran almost passed her destination. Braking on the sidewalk, she stared broodingly at the two-story frame house which had been her home the past seven years. The gingerbread trim was broken away in places, the second-story balcony sagged a little at one end, and the paint was flaking off. The louvered wooden shutters were missing slats and needed to be stripped down to bare wood and refinished, but it was still a handsome, proud old house in her eyes, and she loved every board of it.

Somehow she had to get through to this Jonathan Talbot and convince him to change his mind. He couldn't do this to her. He just *couldn't*.

Propelled by a sense of urgency, she lost no time in using the telephone to locate the whereabouts of the man who seemed to hold her immediate future in his hands. She just hoped he hadn't already left Key West.

Someone of his financial means would undoubtedly be staying either at the Pier House or the Casa Marina, both well-known among those who traveled about the world first-class. She tried the Casa Marina first and didn't have to search further.

"May I speak to Mr. Jonathan Talbot?" she asked briskly in answer to the hotel operator's bored, "Good afternoon. Casa Marina Hotel."

"One moment and I'll see if Mr. Talbot is available. Who may I say is calling, please?"

Fran's self-congratulation was interrupted by the operator's unexpected request for her name. "Francine Bright," she said hesitantly, assailed by a horrible thought. What if Jonathan Talbot refused to see her? The telephone receiver was moist with perspiration from her palm by the time she heard a deep male voice whose crisp enunciation fell hard upon her southerner's ears.

"Yes, Miss Bright. What can I do for you?" The tone was that of a man accustomed to wielding authority. Fran's resolve, fabricated out of a blindly instinctive sense of right, eroded slowly from beneath her feet. Even in those few words, he didn't sound like a man easy to sway.

"Mr. Talbot, I would like to speak to you in person.

24

It's about the houses you've bought, the ones on Whitehead. One of them belonged to my aunt, Liz Todd.'' The request for an interview came out sounding like a demand, made more truculent than she intended by her nervousness. For a long, nerve-shattering moment, she was certain he would refuse to see her.

"I can see you this afternoon, say in an hour? Meet me in the lobby here at the hotel."

Now it was Fran's turn for silence. She was startled at the prospect of having to face him so soon and in such alien surroundings. She had never set foot in the opulent resort hotel, the playground of the very rich, and would prefer to meet him somewhere else where she wouldn't feel quite so out of her element. Better, though, not to risk annoying him or he might refuse to see her at all. Then where would she be?

"Fine, Mr. Talbot. I'll see you in an hour," she said huskily, and hung up before they could change their minds.

As she hurriedly showered and dressed for the interview, her nervousness increased to alarming proportions. She knew the kind of people who lodged at the Casa Marina—they had the patina of money and success all over them. Only a stern reminder to herself that she was just as good as any of those rich snobs gave her the courage she needed to keep her appointment.

After a somewhat rueful inspection of her limited wardrobe, she slipped on a natural-colored cheesecloth blouse and full tiered skirt of paisley design in vibrant hues of pink and purple. As a matter of habit, she wore no jewelry other than rings, those of American Indian-style silver, some inlaid with turquoise and others with golden tiger's eyes or lapis lazuli. With her abundant gold-streaked hair parted down the middle and woven into two heavy braids and her bare feet buckled into leather sandals crafted locally, she was ready.

The parking lot in front of the looming bulk of the

hotel was filled with gleaming automobiles, all emitting an aura of costliness even though Fran wasn't knowledgeable enough about automobiles to recognize them by prestigious manufacturers' names. In front of the awning-shaded entrance, a doorman in gold uniform was extracting leather cases from the trunk of a limousine when Fran walked swiftly by, ignoring the bold challenge in his dark eyes.

Once inside the elegant double doors, with their many small panes of glass, she stopped dead still, gazing around her in stunned awe. The interior of the lobby was grander than anything she'd ever seen firsthand, and far more splendid than she had anticipated. The high vaulted ceiling and ornate lighting fixtures, the richly carved paneling: it all belonged to a bygone era. She was intimidated by the luxuriousness and the vastness of it all.

Across the expanse of polished floor, gracefully arched French doors gave a spectacular vista of emerald green lawns sloping down to immaculate white beach and beyond that the glittering aquamarine of the ocean. To the right was a huge swimming pool surrounded by swimsuit-clad guests sipping drinks under the last rays of the sun. The whole scene had a picture postcard perfection about it, with colors too vivid to be real.

In some strange way Fran perceived herself to be invisible, an insignificant nobody with her nose pressed against the window glass, gazing at royalty in all their splendor. With an unpleasant jolt, she discovered herself to be highly visible as she realized she was being observed with marked disapproval by several carefully groomed dowagers ensconced in low rattan chairs. From their advantageous positions by the high-arched French doors across the lobby, they could view the outside enticements of ocean and beach without venturing beyond the comfort of air conditioning. At the same time, they could keep a hawklike watch on those coming and going through the hotel entrance.

Unaware that she looked disarmingly like some exotic gypsy princess in her colorful attire as she stood poised just inside the polished glass of the imposing entrance doors, Fran comprehended in a flash just how ill-conceived her whole mission was. How could she hope to communicate with someone accustomed to luxury such as this? It was hopeless.

She was pivoting on one foot, about to flee the same way she had come, when a deep voice commanded, "Miss Bright?" Paralyzed, she looked back over her shoulder, her eyes widening in incredulity as she watched a tall man approach her across the mirror bright surface of the floor. It was the same man she'd seen some days ago at Sunset, the one who'd looked so stern and yet had tucked a twenty-dollar bill under the neckline of her blouse. How could she ever forget *him?*

*"You're* Jonathan Talbot?"

If he registered the mixture of disbelief and dismay in her blurted exclamation, there was no sign of it in the cool gray eyes and aloof bearing.

"I hope I didn't keep you waiting." Ignoring the evidence that she had been about to depart without seeing him, he took her by the elbow and steered her up several shallow steps to the left and through solid double doors into the cool, dim interior of a cocktail lounge.

It was quiet, with only a few tables occupied this early in the afternoon. Curious glances in their direction accentuated Fran's intense awareness of the disparity in their dress that made her feel miserably out of place. Jonathan Talbot's manner toward her only made matters worse: judging from his impeccable courtesy, she might have been someone on his own social level, someone who belonged in this luxurious setting.

Seated in a low, deeply-cushioned rattan chair, she

tried to reassemble her poise as the man opposite her focused his attention on the bar, as if using his mental powers to conjure a waiter. Something peremptory in his bearing made her sure he was used to demanding and receiving prompt service.

In the brief respite from those penetrating gray eyes, she studied him. His hair, fashionably styled mid-length, was dark brown, almost black; his features were angular and well-defined, the absence of any excess flesh displaying the strength of bone structure; the sculpted mouth hinting at ruthlessness as well as wry humor. Her preconceived notions about Jonathan Talbot hadn't prepared her for anyone this young and undeniably good-looking. She guessed him to be no more than in his early thirties.

Why hadn't Aunt Liz mentioned that the buyer of her house wasn't an "old codger," as Fran had so disparagingly labeled him? The answer was obvious: Aunt Liz had been in a turmoil those last few days, with more important things on her mind than describing the man who'd purchased her house. And to be honest, Fran had to admit she'd discouraged any discussion of a subject she found deeply painful.

Unexpectedly, the man under her scrutiny turned his head and caught her staring at him. For several seconds she was incapable of speech as the imperturbable eyes flicked over her, arousing the same oddly disconcerting awareness of her femaleness she had experienced that afternoon at Sunset. There was no explaining away as imaginary the crackling electricity in the air between them.

Driven by a compelling urgency to get this meeting over as quickly as possible, she broke the silence, her voice husky with nervousness. "This shouldn't take up much of your time, Mr. Talbot. I know you're probably very busy—"

She broke off as a white-coated waiter paused by

their table, then shook her head when Jonathan Talbot raised his eyebrows inquiringly. "Nothing for me, thank you. I don't drink." She flushed hot with irritation at the mildly ironic question in his faint smile.

"I don't knowingly do *anything* to harm my body," she added stiffly and then wished she hadn't. There was no need for her to defend herself to Jonathan Talbot. Let him think whatever he liked about her.

"Bring the young lady one of your exotic fruit juice concoctions and leave out the rum or whatever. I'll have a double manhattan on the rocks."

She opened her mouth to insist she didn't want anything. She didn't intend to remain there long enough to warrant his ordering a drink for her. But he silenced her with a decisive movement of one shapely hand.

As soon as the waiter was gone, Fran plunged immediately into a less than coherent explanation of her mission, ending with a hurried appeal: "You see, Mr. Talbot, there just aren't that many places kids like us can afford. If you force us to move out of those houses on Whitehead, thirty-some-odd people will be out on the streets with nowhere to sleep."

Breathlessly she watched him for some sign of his reaction, but it was impossible to determine whether she had gotten through to him. His eyes were narrowed speculatively, and he had seemed to be listening closely while she spoke, but he revealed no emotion of any kind.

"What are you suggesting I do, Miss Bright?"

Fran was grateful that the waiter arrived just at that juncture, postponing the necessity for reply. Deep down, she had probably never believed she could change the inevitable flow of events destroying the pleasant tenor of her life, and the straightforward question had come as a surprise. What *was* she suggesting he should do?

Forgetting she hadn't wanted anything to drink, she took up the tall frosted glass and drank deeply without even realizing what she was doing. "Hm, that's very good," she murmured involuntarily. The indulgent amusement in his eyes made her feel every bit of ten years old. To combat the feeling, she sat up very straight, mustering her poise and trying to organize her thoughts.

"Perhaps you could just fix the houses up a little and raise the rent," she suggested hopefully. "At least for a year or so."

"That's no solution, Miss Bright, and you know it. In a year, you and your friends would face precisely the same problem of locating another place to live. In the meantime, three fine old Conch houses would have deteriorated even further."

If he had been curt or overbearing, Fran could have withstood his refusal of her plea. It was the very reasonableness of his tone that stung her. He might have been speaking to a fractious child.

"It isn't *fair!*" she accused, abandoning all tact and caution. "You have no right to force people out of their homes—it's coldblooded and . . . *criminal!*" The last word was a whisper, and without warning her eyes smarted with tears of frustration. She knew now she had failed, and the knowledge erased the last trace of caution. "Just because you have a lot of money—"

His face hardened into resolute planes. "You're without question a very . . . *appealing* ambassador, Miss Bright, but your efforts are somewhat misguided and, I might add, purely selfish. I might rightly deserve the criticism of being 'coldblooded' and 'criminal' if I allowed the houses in question to continue to be abused and neglected the way they have been, for whatever unavoidable reasons."

Tears blurred Fran's vision. She blinked hard and

two great, warm teardrops coursed down her deeply tanned cheeks, forming glistening channels of moistness. Her eyes were brilliant turquoise under curving lashes stuck together in long, wet spikes. Her full, sensitive lips quivered so that she had to bite down on the bottom one with even, white teeth. At some length she managed to summon her voice, rough with emotion.

"I should have known it was useless trying to explain to someone like *you.*" She ignored the tightening of his lips and the ominous light in the watchful gray eyes. "You've probably never been young and free in your whole life. Well, I feel sorry for you, Mr. Talbot, because we—my friends and I—have something you can't buy with all your money. I wouldn't trade places with you for anything in the world—"

"So *here* you are, Jonathan. I've been looking all over for you."

Fran had been so engrossed in her tirade she hadn't noticed anyone approaching their table. Instinct told her even before she looked that the honeyed voice belonged to the sophisticated blonde she'd seen clinging to Jonathan Talbot's arm that previous afternoon at Mallory Square. From the sharp glance she gave Fran now, she evidently remembered the brief encounter, too.

"Have I interrupted something?"

The dulcet sweetness of her tone belied the ice in her gaze as she looked from Fran to the tall man who'd risen courteously at her approach. His face looked annoyed as if he were struggling between the demands of good manners and a more basic honesty.

Well, he needn't worry that Fran would hang around and embarrass him any further by her presence. The appearance of the exquisitely groomed woman with her artificially blonde hair and chic navy pantsuit only emphasized for Fran the utter futility of her endeavor. Her world was untold miles apart from that of Jonathan Talbot and his beautiful wife.

Communication was an impossibility—Fran realized now she had only succeeded in making a fool of herself in front of this urbane man, who must be very amused indeed by her naiveté. Not risking to say another word for fear she would humiliate herself further by bursting into tears, she pushed back her chair and rushed from the room as if pursued by the mythical Furies.

# Chapter Three

Fran's report to her friends the next afternoon at the beach consisted of a terse "Zero" accompanied by a shrug. No one questioned her with any persistence about the details of the interview with the new owner, and she volunteered nothing, realizing none of them had harbored any hopes of her being able to change his mind. Evidently they had all been just humoring her by pretending to believe she might sway him.

Brooding about changing the inevitable was not part of the credo of the young people who migrated to Key West. At this time in their lives, their main purpose was to enjoy today, not worry about tomorrow—which may never come anyway. The water was clear and invigorating. The sun beamed down its tropical warmth. They were young, free, without responsibility. For the moment, what else mattered?

Normally Fran shared this philosophy, but a small core of unhappiness inside her refused to be dissolved. As much as she tried to match the buoyant spirits of her friends, she was unable to rid herself of the despairing feeling that the center of things in her life was disintegrating, that nothing would ever be the same again.

Plagued by restlessness, she left the beach earlier than usual, deciding she would go back to the house and write a letter to Aunt Liz, assuring her everything was fine, even though it wasn't. She wouldn't mention the horror story of that interview with Jonathan Talbot, although it was impossible to banish it from her thoughts.

Today she hadn't taken the extra time to braid her hair, and as she pedaled along, its tangled honey and gold strands streamed out behind her. A pair of faded cutoffs covered the bottoms of her swimsuit, but she had left off the tee shirt. The faded turquoise of her top contrasted with the deep golden brown of her skin.

Unconsciousness of the lovely picture she presented, feminine youth poised on the brink of womanhood, she passed along familiar streets, totally immersed in a mindless enjoyment of her surroundings. A cool breeze brushed her hot skin and lifted the heavy mass of hair from her neck and shoulders. Her soul drank in the color all around her, deep purple and magenta, delicate pinks, whites and reds, with now and then tantalizing glimpses of aqua ocean off to the left.

She wondered idly who the people were standing in front of Aunt Liz's house, staring and pointing at it as if discussing its slightly run-down condition. Then, as she came closer, she recognized the tall, lean figure, its breadth of shoulders and self-confident bearing distinctively belonging to the new owner of the house: *Jonathan Talbot!*

Why was he here? Even though he owned the house now, the present tenants must have some rights of privacy, she reflected indignantly, braking to a halt a few yards from the trio composed of Jonathan Talbot, Joan Ellis, the real estate agent, and a third man who

was a stranger to Fran. Unbeknownst to her, her
expressive features revealed the puzzlement and resentment stirred by their presence outside her home.

Ignoring Jonathan Talbot altogether, Fran smiled at
the other two and inquired politely, "Can I help you?"

The unknown young man was gazing at her with
undisguised admiration and she heard him murmur
something that sounded like "magnificent!" He wasn't
much taller than Fran, who was above average height
for a woman, and was stockily built with a small paunch
swelling his waistline. Dark-rimmed glasses gave him a
scholarly look.

"How fortunate to have you come along like this,
sweetie!" Mrs. Ellis gushed in a tone familiar to Fran,
who suspected the older woman masked her faulty
memory for names with meaningless endearments such
as the one she had just used. "I'd like you to meet Mr.
Talbot and Mr. Bingham. Technically, Mr. Talbot is
your new landlord until the end of the month." She
stressed the last words, looking meaningfully at the tall
man, who showed no reaction. "Mr. Bingham is an
architect and will be in charge of the restoration work
Mr. Talbot plans for this and several other houses he
has purchased."

"It is *indeed* a pleasure? . . ." The stocky young man
took a step toward Fran, smiling an unspoken question,
his eyebrows quirked humorously.

Her husky laughter was spontaneous and unaffected.
"Fran Bright. Actually—*Francine,*" she added, wrinkling her nose in a mock grimace.

Immediately she liked the young architect. Why
couldn't he be the new owner instead of Jonathan
Talbot, who stood there and watched the light exchange, his face as expressionless as the face piece of a
medieval suit of armor.

"Ah, yes, of course . . . Fran." Mrs. Ellis licked lips
heavily encrusted with dark red lipstick. "Mr. Talbot

and Mr. Bingham would like to look through the house in order for Mr. Bingham to begin some advance planning. Since the house is *occupied,*" she gave the last word an exaggerated theatrical intonation, "it would be appropriate for one of the, ah, *tenants* to be present." She seemed to want it made clear that Fran had no special rights because she was the niece of the former owner.

Mr. Bingham looked faintly apologetic, but when Fran's eyes went involuntarily to the face of Jonathan Talbot, she found only impatience there. No doubt he had already wasted enough of his valuable time for one day.

"Help yourself," she said stiffly, wheeling her bicycle past the trio on the sidewalk and lifting it up the steps onto the wide-planked porch, where she chained it to a baluster in the railing. Next, she unlocked the front door with her own key and left it open behind her as she entered the hallway, having every intention of going back to the apartment in which she now lived by herself and leaving Mrs. Ellis to conduct the men through the house.

"Perhaps you would accompany us, Miss Bright."

The low, clipped voice halted her progress and she whirled around and glared at Jonathan Talbot, acknowledging his presence for the first time. His cleanly modeled features looked like a sculpture chiseled into a granite mountainside, but for just an instant she thought she detected a flicker of satisfaction in the depths of his eyes.

Fran opened her mouth to declare hotly that she would *not* accompany them, but Mrs. Ellis interposed smoothly, "When I call Liz tonight and give her the good news that the title is clear and there's nothing now to hold up the act of sale, I'll be sure to mention how *helpful* you've been, sweetie."

Recognizing defeat at this timely reminder of how

important the sale of the house was to Aunt Liz, Fran muttered an ungracious "okay" through clenched teeth, carefully avoiding another glance at Jonathan Talbot. She maintained an aloof silence as she trooped from one room to the next, wishing with chagrin that the boys had been a little neater that morning. Most of the conversation dealt with construction matters and was of no interest to her.

Jonathan Talbot's voice grated on her nerves each time he spoke in that low, crisp tone, and she made it a point to stay as far away from him as possible. Her resentment threatened to boil over during the final part of the tour when they looked through the apartment Fran had shared with Aunt Liz the past seven years. The old furniture and rugs looked sadly worn as she viewed them through the eyes of strangers. No doubt Jonathan Talbot probably thought she lived in a hovel, she reflected scornfully, and wished she had tidied the place up a little more carefully that morning. Thank goodness she was by habit fairly neat and had at least made her bed and picked up her soiled clothes.

Finally it was over. Mrs. Ellis thanked her in the familiar gushing manner, and Mr. Bingham, looking more apologetic than ever, shook her hand and assured her it had been a pleasure to meet her. Only Jonathan Talbot, standing with his hands in his pockets, said nothing as he looked around the room as if cataloging its modest contents. The sight of him, so tall and remote, suddenly was more than Fran could bear. It was intolerable that this total stranger owned not just the house, but all the furnishings as well.

"Don't worry, Mr. Talbot," she said sarcastically, "I won't steal anything when I move out." The barb made no noticeable dent in his self-control.

"Please feel free to take whatever you need for your own personal use. I have no interest in any of it. The remainder will be sold to a secondhand furniture dealer." His courteous voice held an undertone of anger.

Mrs. Ellis looked thoroughly provoked at Fran's rudeness. "Mr. Talbot was *generous* enough to take the furniture off your aunt's hands as a favor when she had to go to Georgia so suddenly. Under the circumstances, she had no need of it."

Fran would have liked to say she herself would have been perfectly capable of disposing of the furniture for Aunt Liz, but deep down she knew the truth. Aunt Liz had been hoping right up to the last that Fran would relent and go to Georgia with her.

"If you don't mind, Mrs. Ellis, Larry, I'd like to have a few words in private with Miss Bright."

Fran heard the words with a combination of shock and uneasiness. What did Jonathan Talbot want to talk to her about? Whatever it was, she didn't care to be left alone with him. From the disapproving expression and pursed lips, Mrs. Ellis evidently shared her misgivings as she swept from the room followed by the architect.

Jonathan Talbot didn't speak at once. He shoved his hands deeper into his pockets, and Fran, avoiding the wintry gray eyes, noticed how the fabric of his tailored slacks molded the hard muscles of his thighs. The observation intensified her discomfiture and she stirred restlessly.

"Are you free this evening?"

Fran couldn't believe her brain had transcribed the right message. "Wh-what?" she demanded incredulously, staring at him.

"We didn't finish our discussion yesterday afternoon. You weren't home all day—I tried several times to telephone you." An undertone in the deep voice combined with a flicker of something indefinable in his eyes awoke in Fran a confused mixture of emotions, among them panic.

"We have *nothing* to talk about—you and I, Mr.

Talbot. Your house will be vacated on time—what else do you want?" The husky timbre of her voice and the impassioned tone made no noticeable impression on the self-contained man.

"I agreed to talk to you yesterday at your request, even though you were a complete stranger with no claim to my time. Don't you think you owe me the same consideration?" The gray eyes probed hers relentlessly. Much as she wanted to refuse to see him that evening, she seemed incapable of speech and he evidently interpreted her silence as acquiescence.

"Good. I'll come back for you in two hours."

"I can't!" she said quickly, his words releasing her from the momentary paralysis.

"Why can't you? Do you have another date?"

Fran felt irrationally as if his eyes were penetrating her brain, making it utterly useless to try to fool him with a lie.

"Not a date, exactly. I promised to go to Sunset." Her eyes evaded his, noticing irrelevantly the rectangles of darker wallpaper where Aunt Liz had removed photographs of Fran. One whole wall had been almost covered with them. She hadn't exactly promised to go to Sunset, but she usually did go.

"We'll go there first, then have dinner."

Fran's eyes widened with disbelief and swung to intersect his, which held both challenge and amusement.

"*You!* You don't mean—you're going to Sunset *with* me?" she gasped.

He eyed the incredulity on her features with a trace of ruefulness and replied dryly, "I promise not to embarrass you in front of your friends."

Memory of an earlier Sunset flashed before her eyes, when this same man had chilled her with the bleakness of his granite eyes and then tucked a twenty-dollar bill under the neckline of her blouse. She could recapture with no effort the brush of his fingertips against her sensitive flesh, the cold blue anger in the eyes of the beautiful blonde at his side. That last image made her stiffen, her own brilliant turquoise eyes shooting sparks of accusation.

"Where is your wife going to be tonight?"

His face went blank and he seemed to be grappling with her words. "My *wife?*" Comprehension dawned. "Ah, you thought Anne . . ." As far as she could see, there was no reason for the satisfaction in his sudden smile, but she caught her breath at the transformation it wrought in his austere features. He was a compellingly attractive man few women would fail to notice, and Fran noted with alarm the way her heartbeat tripped when he smiled at her.

"To set your mind at ease—I'm not married. And now I'd better not keep Mrs. Ellis waiting any longer. Shall I pick you up in two hours, then?"

Before she could agree or make any further protest, he had gone, leaving her to puzzle over the truly astonishing exchange. What could he possibly want to discuss with her? Her mind rejected all possibility that he had any personal interest in her. She was too far removed from his social world, unless . . . did he assume she would be an easy sexual conquest? If so, she would correct that misconception in no uncertain terms when the opportunity arose, she determined grimly.

Later, after a hot shower, Fran stood and surveyed the garments hanging inside the closet that was an addition to the original house. Inexplicably, the screen of her mind flashed the image of a cool, sophisticated blonde, faultlessly groomed and expensively attired. Who *was* she if she wasn't Jonathan Talbot's wife?

Memory of the derision in the unknown woman's assessing gaze made Fran unaccountably dissatisfied with her wardrobe, and then irritated at herself for such absurdity. Finally, she pulled off the hanger her favorite dress, a sundress of loosely-woven cotton, the top severely plain with wide straps across the shoulder forming a square neckline in the front and the back. The waist fit snug and the skirt swirled out to circular fullness around the calves. The color was the same neutral tone as unbleached muslin except for the layers of ruffles of vibrant orange, yellow and red at the bottom of the skirt.

The simplicity of style and color emphasized the smooth brownness of her arms, neck and shoulders, and the willowy grace of her tall, slender figure. Her hair, brushed until it was soft and shining, was held back from her face by a braided band lavishly embroidered in metallic threads of orange, yellow and gold.

After she was dressed, a process which took amazingly little time since she used no makeup, Fran studied her reflection in the mirror with a newly critical eye. She wasn't chic and fashionable like Jonathan Talbot's blonde companion, but then she had no desire to be anything other than herself. She dressed to please herself, not some fashion editor in New York City. Darn Jonathan Talbot, anyway, for disrupting her life and raising thoughts that never would have occurred to her before now!

The residue of resentment lit sparks in her blue eyes and gave a firm set to her jawline when she greeted the man from Maine a few minutes later. He, too, had changed clothing, discarding the formality of his suit for more casual attire. A glance at the cut of fabric of his soft gray slacks and navy velour pullover was enough to attest to their costliness. The sight of him, tall and cleanly masculine, standing there and smiling down at her, disconcerted Fran by stirring her with the last thought she ever expected to feel in his presence: regret. For one crazy moment, she almost wished she were not so separated from him by differences of background, education and experience. What would it be like to feel confident and relaxed in his company—to know he was attracted to her?

Appalled at the exhilaration these fancies produced, Fran deliberately shattered the spell holding her captive. "I can't believe you're really *serious* about the two of us going out to eat together." Her voice firmly raised between them multiple barriers of social position, age and lifestyle.

He frowned with annoyance. "Oh? I didn't realize I left any doubt about my intentions."

She hated herself for the telltale warmth suffusing her face, and also for the inability to hold his penetrating gaze, which cut right through the flimsiness of her pretense. Every time she encountered this man, she was made more aware of an indomitable quality that made crossing his will, *or* fooling him, a futile effort.

"Sorry the prospect of a few hours in my company has so little appeal. Nevertheless . . . shall we get started?"

They were soon walking along among groups of people headed in the same general direction of the concrete pier. Fran grew quiet, once more awkwardly conscious of the man beside her. All the Sunset "regulars" who came to entertain or to watch their friends knew her. They'd be amazed to see her in the company of a man, especially someone so patently out of her class.

Sensing her discomfiture, if not the underlying reason for it, Jonathan Talbot ordered in a low, amused voice, "Relax. I don't have a camera hidden away in my pocket," as if she were embarrassed at being seen in the company of someone who might be taken for a tourist.

She didn't answer as they climbed the steps up to the pier and merged with the crowds of people milling around in the anxiety not to miss anything. With an agility born of practice, she edged her way to the inside of a crowd surrounding a trio engaged in an elaborate comedy act featuring a mime made up to resemble Charlie Chaplin. Momentarily relaxed in the assurance of having slipped away from her escort, she applauded enthusiastically as the mime executed a sensational fall.

Suddenly she stiffened and sucked in her breath sharply as a firm hand came to rest lightly on her shoulder. Her head tilted back and she looked straight into enigmatic gray eyes. Doggedly she tried to ignore the closeness of him in the eager, pressing crowd. Normally her attention would have been fully arrested by the efforts of the young performers and the responses of the crowd, but she was more keenly aware at that moment of the hand which entangled itself gently in the long loose strands of her hair.

In desperation she turned sideways and began to maneuver to the outside of the group of onlookers, but the hand only slipped from her shoulder to curve protectively against her slim waist. With strangely heightened senses, she walked slowly beside him, viewing the familiar scene around them. Any minute she expected him to suggest they leave, but he seemed totally receptive to her direction.

At the far end of the pier, they watched the same group of musicians she'd taken pity upon that previous Sunset when she'd come face to face for the first time with the man beside her now. Wincing at the roughness of their execution of a favorite number of hers, she wondered if he also was remembering that jolting first encounter. He removed all doubt when he bent close and murmured in her ear, "They don't show much improvement, do they?" A little shiver slid down her spine at the warmth of his breath brushing her cheek.

She didn't protest when he turned her away from the unskilled efforts of the musicians and guided her to the edge of the pier facing the glowing orb of the sun as it rested for a breathtaking moment on the gilded ocean.

43

Side by side they stood and watched as the brilliant red ball sank from view, leaving behind a rose-tinted horizon.

Fran had seen the same sight hundreds of times, but it never failed to arouse a sense of awe and gratitude. Tonight she wasn't inclined to join the applause, which somehow profaned the quiet beauty of what she'd just experienced.

The usual flurry following the setting of the sun brought her back to the present. Suddenly, she was aware of curious looks in her direction. In the dusky light she could see her companion's half smile and knew he could read her thoughts and was conscious of her discomfiture.

Without speaking, he steered her toward a set of steps leading down into the parking lot and walked beside her toward Front Street. She searched her mind for something to say and came up with a blank. Then curiosity got the better of her as he turned left on Front Street.

"Where are you going?"

"I thought we'd have dinner at A & B Lobster House, if that's all right with you."

She didn't answer. Of course she knew the restaurant's reputation as one of the best places to eat in Key West. The decor was plain, but the prices exceeded what she and her friends could afford.

The two-story building, which judging from its stark white exterior might have been a warehouse, was located at the end of Front Street, right on the edge of the harbor. To the left was a ghostly outline of a replica of a famous Spanish galleon, open to the public for a small entrance fee during the day. The restaurant occupied the second story of the building and over-looked the harbor. A shrimp fleet was being moored to the far right.

They rode the small, stuffy elevator to the second

floor and passed through the bar into the restaurant, where they were greeted by the hostess and shown to a windowside table at the right corner. After one speculative glance at Fran, the hostess concentrated all her smiling attention upon Jonathan Talbot, who was plainly accustomed to this kind of deference.

There was an awkward moment for Fran when she realized he assumed she was familiar with the restaurant's fare. "What do you recommend?" he asked when the waitress had come and presented them with menus.

"I've never eaten here before," she answered with characteristic candor and then read the incredulous expression on his face, realizing anew the great gulf separating them. She shrugged defensively. "This place is a little out of my price range, Mr. Talbot."

While he studied the menu, she glanced around in surprise at the mellow tones of a young singer. She hadn't noticed him when she entered the dining room because he was positioned in a corner just inside the entrance. He had lived for several months in her aunt's house when he first came to Key West, and she hadn't seen him for some time.

"Friend of yours?"

She wondered at the sharpness of Jonathan Talbot's voice as he looked up and noted her expression. "That's Brian Brandon. I wondered what ever happened to him. He's really good."

"Is he?"

Her eyebrows drew together in faint puzzlement. "You can decide for yourself after you've listened to him." Something deep in his eyes caused a strange tension inside her, and she glanced away from him toward the window, as though interested in the view of the darkening harbor.

"Let's get one thing straight for the record, Mr. Talbot. I don't sleep around. Not that it would be any

45

of your business if I did." She kept her head stiffly averted, but could feel his probing gaze on her profile.

"Why don't you perform regularly at Sunset?"

Her head swung in amazed response to the calm question. From the expression on his face, she might never have made that impassioned declaration.

"Because I have a regular job, such as it is."

A frown of puzzlement cut twin lines between his eyebrows. "I don't see what that has to do with it."

Fran didn't understand why he was even mildly curious, either, but the subject seemed safe enough, and as she answered him, the strange tension slowly ebbed.

"Entertaining the tourists at Sunset is the only way some kids can support themselves when they first get to Key West. It's not fair for somebody like me, somebody who has a job and a place to live—" She broke off as she realized she had spoken from years of habit. No longer did she have a place to live, not for long, anyway.

"What kind of job do you have?" He showed no awareness of the slip.

"I work in the Lemon Tree Boutique, off Duval. It doesn't pay much, just minimum wage, but it's easy and kind of fun. Most of the customers are kids my own age. I get a discount on everything I buy." She glanced down at the sundress she was wearing.

"How old are you?"

Fran hesitated, tempted for a second to make some comment about this pointless interrogation. Then she realized he was probably as much at a loss for topics of conversation as she was.

"I'll soon be twenty."

His eyes widened a fraction and one eyebrow elevated. "You seem much younger. And when your aunt spoke of you the morning I met with her, she made you sound like a sixteen-year-old."

"You talked about me with my aunt?" Fran was incredulous at this revelation and then slowly the truth sank in. Now she understood why Jonathan Talbot had wanted to talk to her tonight, why he was asking her all these questions. Poor Aunt Liz had undoubtedly poured out all her worries about leaving Fran behind in Key West and Jonathan Talbot was feeling guilty about forcing a defenseless young girl out on the streets.

"I can take care of myself, Mr. Talbot. I have a good job offer to sing with a band. If it works out, I'll be able to quit the Lemon Tree."

Strangely enough he didn't look at all reassured by that news, and his reply might have been a quotation of Aunt Liz herself. "That's hardly a suitable job for a young girl—woman like yourself."

Fran paid scant attention to his correction of *girl* to *woman*. She was too indignant over his sheer brass. "If it weren't for *you*, I wouldn't have to take it!" she snapped angrily.

The waitress chose that moment to reappear and ask if they were ready to order. Fran hadn't even looked at the menu, which seemed a blank as she stared down at it.

"What's the specialty of the house?" he asked pleasantly of the waitress and upon hearing her suggestions, wanted to know if those dishes appealed to Fran. At that moment, Fran would have agreed to anything—food seemed to be of such trivial importance. She wanted the waitress to leave so that the conversation could be resumed.

His manners, faultless without the least hint of effort, were all the more noticeable to Fran, who was not accustomed to such male courtesy. Among her own contemporaries, the finer points of etiquette were definitely absent. The eyes of other women in the restaurant followed Jonathan Talbot as he spoke softly to Fran. No doubt they all envied her and wondered

47

what a man like that could see in *her*, Fran reflected grimly, nevertheless holding her head at a proud angle.

She ate with relish, finding each course as delicious as the last. For each of them there was a fresh salad, and a cup of conch chowder, rich with cream and chunks of chewy meat and potato and onion. Following the soup course was conch fritters, deep-fried to a golden color, and then the main course of filet of grouper and baked potato. The grouper was tender and sweet with none of the strong fishy flavor of frozen seafood.

Jonathan Talbot raised his eyebrows humorously when Fran declared herself unable to eat another bite, not even the Key Lime pie, a dessert specialty in Key West. "You sure? Coffee?"

She hesitated and then nodded acceptance of the coffee. A few minutes later he watched her add a liberal portion of cream to her cup, turning the liquid a pale color.

"How do you manage to stay so slender?" The frank amusement was mingled with something so similar to admiration she was confused and taken aback. To combat the reaction, she told him about her passion for physical exercise, albeit not on any rigid schedule: jogging, swimming, bike riding, miles of walking and yoga stretch exercises.

"Besides," she admitted with a disarming smile, "I don't often get a chance to eat in a place that serves food this good."

After that, he seemed to withdraw into his own thoughts, leaving Fran prey to a sudden restlessness. Glancing around idly at the other diners, she heaved a little sigh quite unconsciously and immediately felt the weight of his scrutiny. What was he thinking about that made him look so solemn, she wondered uneasily, but his words gave her no clue.

"Ready to go?"

She was definitely ready to leave the restaurant, to be

rid of his company and the probing scrutiny of his gray eyes, which seemed to see far too much. After tonight, she probably wouldn't see him again, and it was all for the best that she didn't. He didn't belong in her world, which excluded ambition and pursuit of material possessions and put a premium on day-to-day enjoyment of life.

He was silent as he walked beside her along narrow, dimly lighted streets, and she was free to relax and surrender her senses to the demands of her surroundings. The night air was fragrant with the blossoms of vines and shrubs growing inside the picket fences they passed. A breeze blowing off the ocean brought the tangy salt air to her nostrils. Idly she reached up as they walked beneath the overhanging branches of an orchid tree and plucked a twig laden with delicate miniature orchids.

Brushing the silken petals along her cheek, she wondered as she so often did the last few weeks: how can I bear to give all this up? This very special beauty and serenity. If Aunt Liz understood the depth of her attachment to Key West, she wouldn't expect her to go back to Georgia and be reminded continually of the bleak, dreary life she had known there with her father.

Unconsciously her steps quickened with the anxiety of these thoughts, and one foot caught on a gnarled root extending over the edge of the sidewalk. She might have pitched headlong if the man beside her hadn't moved so quickly and caught her in his arms. Her heart pounded wildly, at first because she had come so close to falling and then because he didn't release her once her balance was restored. She could feel the answering thud from his own chest next to her body.

Before she could extricate herself from the closeness that made her alarmingly conscious of his tall, rugged length, he took her totally by surprise by lowering his mouth to hers. It was in no way a savage, demanding kiss, but exploratory at first and then coaxing. His lips were firm and knowledgeable, and for the first shocked instants, Fran liked the feel of them on hers, which of their own volition became soft and clinging.

Then her brain awakened and telegraphed an appalling message: not only was she allowing a strange man to kiss her, she was responding with pleasure. She was behaving as wantonly as her father had predicted she would, following in the pattern established by the first woman, and more recently by her own mother. Revulsion at herself and anger at this man who had caused her to act in this way gave Fran a superhuman strength she didn't really need, since Jonathan Talbot released her immediately when she cried out an anguished "Let me go!" and jerked away from him.

She felt his scrutiny in the darkness as she stood a few feet away from him, trembling so violently her teeth chattered. "You shouldn't have done that!" she said in a tone low with desperation. He muttered something under his breath before he took a step closer as though he were going to take her in his arms again.

"Don't you touch me!" she warned shrilly, whirling around to face him like a threatened beast of the wild. "You think all women are like that, but they're not. *I'm* not!"

"What are you talking about?" His voice held restrained impatience and the sound of it brought Fran to her senses. Her heartbeat was slowing and the sickening dizziness was subsiding. Now she wanted nothing but to escape from this man's presence and have the opportunity to be alone and sort out what had just happened.

"Forget it," she said tersely and began walking fast.

"I won't forget it," he said furiously, his long legs making it easy for him to catch up with her and match her rapid pace.

"I don't know what you thought my intentions were

back there," he said after a while, his tone even now, "but I was *not* assaulting you. I apologize if I offended you."

Fran closed her ears to the deep resonance of his voice. "Your apology is accepted. Now if you don't mind, Mr. Talbot, I'd appreciate it if you'd just leave me alone. I can find my own way home. I do it all the time."

He drew in a sharp breath and muttered as if to himself, "What have I gotten myself into?"

Fran had no inkling of what he was talking about and no intention of pursuing that subject or any other with him. Using her knowledge of every street in Key West, she took the shortest route possible to the house on Whitehead, not uttering a word until she paused briefly on the sidewalk.

"Thank you for the dinner, Mr. Talbot. Goodbye." Sounding like the least talented of actresses reciting words that meant nothing, she spoke these parting words and left him standing there.

# Chapter Four

"Okay, honey, give it all you got out there tonight. Remember what I told you, the customers don't pile in here just to hear your pretty voice. The boss is going to be out in the audience later on, and he'll probably ask you to join him and his friends for a drink."

Fran despised the heavy warmth of Jack Braden's paw on her shoulder, and she schooled herself not to jerk away from him as her instincts dictated. He was the manager of the Black Pig and as her immediate boss seemed to think his position endowed him with the right to touch her with casual familiarity.

She knew what he meant by "give it all you got." He and Bob Silver, the leader of the band, had harped constantly on the subject. They wanted her to seduce the audience with her body—to strut and twist and put herself on display up on the stage until you could burn down the building with the sexual electricity crackling the air.

It was almost a week now since she began the job as female vocalist with the Silver-Stringed Vagrants, and she hated every minute of that time up on the lighted dais. Not that she minded singing and playing various instruments for the enjoyment of other people, because she didn't. Her musical aptitude made it easy for her to give a pleasant rendition of almost any popular song, and to play almost any instrument she picked up. What she did mind were the coarse remarks that floated to her ears now and then and made her burn with humiliation, the hands reaching out insistently when she tried to walk through the crowded room to join a table of her friends during an intermission, the male voices cajoling and begging her to stop at their table and have a drink with them.

And now tonight, Jack Braden telling her she would be expected to have a drink with the boss and his friends. What else would she be expected to do?

When the final performance was over that night, after two encores, Fran reflected bitterly upon the wild response of the audience. It just proved how unimportant she was to them as a real person, because that certainly hadn't been *her* out there. She had removed herself entirely from what she was doing, feeling like a separate entity watching a total stranger perform. She just hoped Jack Braden and Bob Silver were happy now that she had given them what they'd been demanding of her. Personally, she felt degraded and sick to her stomach. All she wanted now was to slip out the back way and go somewhere where she could be alone.

"Fran! Don't run off. The boss wants to buy you a drink."

She stiffened and then slumped tiredly, turning around slowly to face Jack Braden. "Jack, I—" she began and then stopped as she became aware of a man who appeared just behind the manager. Jonathan Talbot! Had he been out there in the audience, tonight of all nights? Had he seen that disgusting exhibition? The thought sickened her.

"Are you ready, Fran?" he said grimly, causing Jack to start and look over his shoulder. Surprisingly, the manager didn't make any further issue of her joining the boss at his table, but turned away and left her standing there facing Jonathan Talbot.

"Were you here?" she asked abruptly.

"I was here," he said brusquely. "Let's get out of here." Taking her arm, he propelled her firmly through the passageway leading to the rear exit, ignoring signs that announced EMPLOYEES ONLY.

He kept her arm as they left the noise of nightlife on Duval Street, and were soon walking along silent residential streets. After a while she noticed their present direction would bring them eventually to the public beach adjoining the grounds of the Casa Marina. At the moment she really didn't care—about anything. She was tired, so tired.

They passed the deserted public tennis courts, ghostly in the late night quietness, and crossed the street to City Beach, disregarding signs proclaiming CLOSED TO VISITORS AFTER 10:00 P.M. Fran felt the crunch of brittle particles of sand under her feet, and reached down to slip off her shoes. Pulling free of his hand, she walked across to the water's edge. The cold, wet lap of the tide against her bare feet and the silvery mantle of moonlight transforming sand and sea into a world of magic gradually helped to ease the distress in Fran's soul.

She was awakening from some dreadful nightmare into a familiar world of serenity and beauty. This was where she belonged—Key West—whatever the cost. Leaving would be like wrenching the myriad vinelike roots of the banyan tree from its friendly, supportive soil.

"Is it worth it?"

The curt question made her jump, coming as it did from so close by. She had almost forgotten Jonathan Talbot's presence.

"Is what worth it?" They both heard the defensive note in her voice, and knew she had understood the meaning of his cryptic question.

"Is staying here in this expensive resort area worth selling yourself?"

The contempt in his voice hurt, but she was much too honest to contest his condemnation of what she had forced herself to do tonight up on that stage. She felt the same way. But the defiance in her reply told him *he* had no right to criticize her.

"I have nowhere else to go. I've never lived anywhere but here and—Georgia." She almost choked on the last word as if it had a vile taste.

"Why not go back there then? Your aunt seemed genuinely fond of you. Wouldn't she agree to have you live with her?"

"Of course, she would. She's hoping I'll come to my senses and realize I can't afford to stay here. But I won't go back there—*I won't!*" The weariness in her voice changed to vehemence on the last words, and she drew a sharp look from her companion.

"What was there so horrible about your life in Georgia, Fran?"

They had begun walking slowly along the edge of the water, and she was making little kicking motions in the curling tide. Perhaps if she hadn't felt so defeated, she might have told him it was none of his business, but for reasons she didn't comprehend, she suddenly wanted him to understand.

"It wasn't horrible in the way you might mean—my father never beat me or mistreated me physically. It was just that for twelve dreary years, I lived in a house where it was a crime to laugh or joke or—or be happy."

"You don't mention your mother."

55

"I never knew her." Fran hesitated, and then decided to go ahead and tell him. "She left when I was just a baby. According to my father, she ran away with another man. I don't know whether she did or not. After I was older, I didn't really blame her, whatever her reasons, for leaving him. I hope she was happy wherever she went."

"I take it your father was bitter toward her." Jonathan's voice revealed nothing of what he might be thinking of this tale of domestic unhappiness.

"I guess he was. He seemed bitter about everything to me." Fran was deliberately evasive here. She didn't care to get into the subject of her father's views on women. She could hear him now, thundering at her: "Women are all tramps! Every last one of them!"

Disturbed at the memory, she stopped and turned her back to Jonathan, looking out at the dark sea. Without warning, his hands clasped her shoulders and she was stirred by a powerful longing to lean back against him, followed by self-loathing for her weakness.

"Don't touch me!" she whispered harshly, twisting away from him, her breathing audible in the disturbing silence that followed.

"Why shouldn't I touch you?" There was an odd undertone in his voice, as if he already half-suspected the answer. Even as Fran blurted a reply, she knew she was revealing far more than she wanted to.

"I don't want any man to touch me—*ever!* My father was wrong about me!" She saw him rake a hand through his hair as though he were angry, and he sounded so when he spoke.

"I think I'm beginning to see. . . ."

Whatever it was that he was beginning to understand, he didn't choose to explain it to her, but suggested that the time was very late and she should be getting home to bed. Fran agreed readily. She was dead

56

on her feet, tired not just physically, but emotionally as well. Already she was regretting having let down her guard the way she had tonight. Not one of her friends knew the background she had revealed to Jonathan Talbot. Not even Aunt Liz had probed as deeply as he had.

"Have you found a place to live yet?"

His question effectively restored them to their former roles as people in worlds that didn't touch. Fran was relieved, and sought to increase the distance separating them.

"Sort of. One of the girls at the Lemon Tree has said I can move in with her until I find something permanent. Some of the others in your houses haven't been so lucky." The accusing note in her voice reminded him *he* was the culprit dislodging innocent people from their living quarters.

"How many haven't been able to locate another place to rent?"

"The majority of them haven't. The ones who have are mostly like me, having to impose on somebody for heaven knows how long."

He made no reply, and she felt a touch of compunction for her stinging tone until she reminded herself he deserved to feel a little guilt for interfering in other people's lives, even if it was just business for him.

"Goodnight, Fran. I'll see you tomorrow."

They had arrived at her house and were standing on the porch when he made these parting words and departed abruptly, leaving her to stare after him. It occurred to her for the first time that he had dropped the formality and called her Fran several times that evening. She hadn't addressed him by name at all. *Jonathan*. She tried out the name, saying it aloud. He was the only person she'd ever known by that name, and somehow it suited him. It had a solid, authoritative ring.

What had he meant by saying he would see her tomorrow?

Fran was far too busy the first half of the next day to give any thought to that post-midnight conversation with Jonathan and its revelations about her past. She awakened to the buzz of the alarm clock and dragged herself out of bed to dress for work. Until she was sure the singing job would work out, she didn't dare give up the job at the boutique.

The shop was swarming with customers from the time she arrived until she took her lunch break at noon. Frequently, she rode her bicycle back home and ate something there, but today she didn't have the energy to slap a sandwich together. What she desperately needed, though, was somewhere quiet to get a light meal. Pondering this problem, she stepped out the front door of the Lemon Tree onto the sidewalk and looked undecidedly in both directions. For a moment, she couldn't believe her eyes when she saw Jonathan Talbot striding toward her.

"Good. I thought I might have missed you," he called out, and she looked involuntarily over her shoulder to make sure he wasn't talking to someone else.

"Have lunch with me?" he asked, coming to a stop beside her, his casual tone making it sound as if his arriving at the Lemon Tree just as she was leaving on her lunch break was an ordinary, everyday occurrence.

"Where?" she said weakly.

His gray eyes skimmed her face. Faint circles of tiredness under the eyes accentuated their intense blueness. "I know a quiet place a few blocks from here."

He had said the magic words, and she went willingly

with him, grateful as she had been last night, when he intervened at the Black Pig, for his decisiveness and air of capability. A few minutes later, she faced him across a small table in the corner of a restaurant whose exclusive atmosphere and higher prices made it less crowded and noisy than the sandwich shops. Grateful for the cool, relaxing ambiance, Fran rested her elbows on the table so that she could support her chin on clasped hands. Closing her eyes, she breathed a deep sigh.

The food revived her energy to some extent. She ate every morsel of a huge chef salad and then had dessert, a wedge of Key Lime pie. Jonathan made no comment on her appetite this time. In fact, he said very little during the meal, a fact for which she was grateful, since she didn't feel like conversation.

"Feel better?"

She smiled an affirmative answer as she settled back in her chair and watched him cradle his coffee cup in hands that were lean, well-shaped and suggestive of strength.

"How is your architect coming along with the plans for your houses?" she asked conversationally.

"Larry? He's more than just my architect. He's one of my oldest and best friends. To answer your question, he will soon be ready to get the workmen started on one of the houses." He drained the coffee cup and set it down. "Which brings me to the subject I want to discuss with you."

Fran was surprised and more than a little curious, not having been aware until now that he had invited her to lunch with any purpose in mind.

"I've been thinking over what you suggested that afternoon you came to the hotel, and I've concluded you have a point. It's hardly feasible to begin immediate restoration on all five of the houses I've purchased. Therefore, I've decided to allow the tenants in the three houses that are presently occupied to remain there until the end of the year."

Fran listened, too stunned to speak.

"In the meantime, no new tenants would be allowed to move in, and the rent will have to be raised enough to cover cleaning and routine maintenance expenses now that the previous owners no longer live on the premises."

"Oh, Jonathan! That's wonderful news!" Fran breathed, finally recovering her voice. Her eyes glowed at this unforeseen good turn of events.

"Better hear me out," he inserted dryly. "The one requirement is that *you* move out of the house you're living in and put yourself in my care for that same period of time, almost a year."

"Wh-what? You must be out of your mind!" she gasped.

"I may well be." His voice was ironic. "If you agree, you will have to adhere to certain conditions."

"I'll bet." The suspicion in her tone and face brought a flicker of amusement to her companion's eyes.

"And not what you're so obviously thinking. I don't find it in the least necessary to take advantage of inexperienced young virgins."

The chiding note in his voice brought a sharp stab of resentment to Fran's breast, followed by a mental image of a chic blonde with ice cold blue eyes. No doubt *that* was the kind of woman he preferred.

"What conditions?" she asked skeptically. Not that she had any intentions of turning herself over to him, as he put it. The nerve!

"I've leased a house for Larry Bingham to use as his working and living headquarters. You would live there, too. It would be a perfectly respectable arrangement, since three permanent staff members, two of them mature women, live on the premises. You would quit the singing job immediately, and preferably begin some kind of educational training to qualify you to earn a living." He hesitated, as if choosing the next words with great care. "You would also agree to associate with totally different people: people with some goals and purpose in life. In short, what I'm suggesting is that you explore a set of values very different from your own at present."

Fran was overwhelmed with disbelief. She must be hallucinating, and would soon return to reality and find she had imagined all this.

"You're *crazy!*" she managed to get out finally. "I have no intention of giving up my friends *or* my 'set of values,' which I happen to think are perfectly good. The answer is *no!*"

His chiseled features reminded her of the granite monument of a Civil War general in the town square of her former home town in Georgia. "That, of course, is your decision to make. But I urge you to give it some serious thought. If you refuse my terms, you'll be directly responsible for turning your friends out onto the street when they could have the extra time they need to find other living accommodations. And you, unless you come to compromise your present personal standards, will eventually be forced to leave Key West."

The words were like sharp surgical tools cutting into her. Their truth was so irrefutable. Right now it was time for her to go back to work for another two hours. Then she would go straight home and fall into bed until it was time to get ready to go to the club, where once again she would have to suffer Jack Braden's heavy-handed familiarity, the whistles and yells from the audience which grew rowdier with the lateness of the hour and the quantity of alcohol consumed, the insistent demands from customers to socialize with them—

Was Jonathan Talbot right? Would she eventually compromise her personal standards of conduct if she stayed in nightclub entertaining?

"What if I changed my mind before the year is up?" she asked gravely.

Some tension in him eased, and she realized he had been sitting there silently while she wandered through her own private torture chamber.

"You'll always be free to change your mind, if you find the circumstances impossible to tolerate. After all, you're not entering a prison." His mouth twisted in a wry, familiar smile she found reassuring. "You may even learn to like it."

Fran looked down at her hands, which were twisted together on the table surface in front of her. "Why are you doing this?" When there was no immediate answer, she looked up and found him watching her. "Why, Jonathan? What's in this for you?" She wasn't even aware she had addressed him by his given name for the second time.

His attractive mouth twisted into a half smile, making her intensely conscious of his masculine appeal.

"Call it my own little rehabilitation project."

The light, almost playful tone brought an odd constriction to her chest. Why, she didn't know. Certainly she didn't expect or wish him to declare himself bowled over by her female attractions. If he had, she wouldn't even consider his strange proposal, and she *was* considering it. In fact, in her mind she had already accepted it. Instinctively, she knew she could trust him to keep his word; he wouldn't ask her to do anything to compromise her principles. And what he suggested seemed an immediate solution to her most pressing problems.

"Well, Fran? What's it to be?"

"I'll have to call Aunt Liz first and see what she has to say."

They both knew her own answer now, and beneath his controlled exterior was the merest hint of triumph. For Fran, there was puzzlement over his motivations and apprehension at the uncertainty of what her future held in store.

# Chapter Five

"Hey, that's nice!"

"Thank you, Larry. Actually, *you're* nice."

The warmth in Fran's voice revealed the depth of her sincerity as she sat down opposite Larry Bingham at the round glass-topped table on the patio. His compliment had been intended for the new sundress she wore, a delectable lime green garment made of a fabric so light and cool it was almost like wearing nothing. The admiring light in Larry's warm, brown eyes behind the dark-rimmed glasses was for far more, however, than just the dress.

What would she have done without him the last twelve weeks? She was about to speak that thought aloud when Joanna came out with lunch. Fran still hadn't accustomed herself to being waited on. Those first days after moving into the lovely old Key West house had been times of great awkwardness for her, especially when she discovered nothing was expected of her in the way of housework or cooking. She didn't even have to make her own bed unless she wished to do so. The two sisters, Joanna and Maria, ran the household so efficiently that to offer help was ludicrous.

From what Fran had been able to learn from their extremely sparse conversational offerings, both women were spinsters in their forties and natives of Key West. They, along with their brother Joseph, the gardener, had taken care of this house through a succession of owners for the past twenty-five or thirty years. When Jonathan Talbot leased the Garrett House, as it was called after the original owner and builder, the staff of three were included in the lease agreement.

Surely the two laconic sisters must have felt some curiosity about the relationships among those who now occupied the house. Most of the time there was just Larry Bingham and Fran, with the occasional presence of Jonathan Talbot. But from the impassive demeanor of the staff of three, the household might have been the most conventional in Key West.

"Busy at the shop this morning?"

Larry's pleasantly deep male voice brought Fran back to the present, making her realize she hadn't even begun to eat the appetizing salad placed in front of her. It looked like a mixture of shrimp and lobster.

She nodded an affirmative to his question and picked up her fork. "Hm-m-m. This looks good." After a few bites, she continued. "To answer your question, I've been unpacking a new shipment. Eleanor's stock is sure different from what I sold at the Lemon Tree."

The job offer to work in Eleanor Caronne's nationally known dress shop had come just days after Fran moved into Garrett House. There could be little doubt that Jonathan was responsible for it since Eleanor, as it turned out, was another old friend of his. But she was undeniably businesslike in her treatment of Fran, working her hard so that Fran earned her good wages. She insisted, though, that Fran dress in the clothes she sold in the shop, making that possible by giving her a drastically reduced price, explaining that as one of the fringe benefits of working for her.

"Jonathan's coming in some time this afternoon."

Fran sensed that Larry expected some reply to his announcement, which had accelerated her pulse alarmingly, even if it hadn't dented her outward poise. By now she was becoming practiced at pretending Jonathan's presence didn't disconcert her as it invariably did.

"He's probably coming to check on the rehab program," she said flippantly. Between herself and Larry, she habitually referred to herself and her current life with light mockery. It was a defense mechanism to conceal the puzzlement and confusion which sometimes plagued her, even after twelve weeks. It was still beyond her comprehension why Jonathan had interfered in her life as he had done, considering that he was so rarely here to see his "Great Experiment." She could be sure now that he had no personal interest in her.

Some little inflection in her voice had caused Larry Bingham to look closely at the clouded face of the lovely girl opposite him. For she was indeed lovely in her transformation. The first day Larry had seen her outside the old house on Whitehead, he had been stunned by her natural beauty and inherent grace. Since that time, she had taken on an aura of sophistication, a metamorphosis supervised by Eleanor Caronne, and one which caused him a tinge of regret for what was lost, as well as great pleasure in the end result.

Gone were the ragged cutoffs and roughly crafted leather sandals, the sacklike cotton skirts and blouses in brilliant clashing colors, the long heavy braids. To liken the change to a butterfly emerging from a drab chrysalis was a faulty parallel, for Fran had been startlingly beautiful before. But now she wore expensive clothes which showed off her superb young body, and her hair had been shortened and styled to frame her face and fall just below the shoulders in soft waves and curls.

Some vestiges of her old life remained in her passion for exercise. Larry knew she frequently rose very early and jogged several miles. She also swam daily in the large private swimming pool. He hadn't known about the yoga exercises until one night he complained of tension in his neck and shoulders, and Fran demonstrated several simple exercises to relax the bunched muscles.

While she no longer covered her slender hands with the turquoise and silver rings, she still wore them, one or two at a time, as if she needed to retain something of her former rather Bohemian tastes. As far as Larry was concerned, Fran could wear anything she chose and still eclipse all the women he'd ever known. He'd have willingly done the modern equivalent, whatever that happened to be, of walking over red-hot stones for her.

Yet it wasn't just her exceptional beauty that made him adore her. She was sweet, and by that he didn't mean cloying and artificial or inane. There was a directness and innocence of spirit about her that made him want to protect her from anything sordid or hurtful she might encounter. But right now he knew he had to conceal the way he felt. She needed him as a friend, not a suitor. And besides, there was Jonathan—but he preferred not to pursue his thoughts in that direction.

"How are the classes?" His crisp northerner's voice betrayed no hint of what he had been thinking.

"Pretty interesting—now that I've gotten over resenting having to go at all," she admitted honestly. He knew, of course, that part of Jonathan's program of change was for her to continue her education. She was attending afternoon classes at the local junior college.

Currently, she was taking basic freshman courses, such as English and history.

"It's hard to believe I lived right here in Key West for so long and managed to learn so little about its history, which is quite fascinating."

He nodded encouragement without interrupting, content to enjoy the liquid softness of her southern accent as she elaborated. "I always thought those funny little lookouts on top of some of the old houses were a neat idea, but I didn't realize they had such a practical purpose."

In her enthusiasm, she either forgot or overlooked the fact that as an architect employed in the restoration of five old Key West houses, Larry was thoroughly versed in the architectural history of the area. He knew the widow's or captain's walk had been used originally to sight shipwrecks on the reef off Key West. Back in the days when salvaging was a lucrative business, the first captain to reach a wrecked ship had major salvage rights. As a consequence, the homes in Key West during those days had contained the finest the world had to offer in furniture, silver, porcelain and other expensive commodities.

From the interested expression on Larry's face, he might have been learning something totally new when Fran informed him that the builders of the Conch style houses were, for the most part, ship's carpenters, and did not work from formal sets of plans.

"They incorporated ideas they saw in the ports they visited all over the world and used the same skills and techniques they'd learned building and repairing ships. Instead of nails, they used wooden pins so that the houses actually sway and 'give' a little in hurricane winds. That's why so many have managed to survive violent tropical storms.

"The way the houses were built was so practical,"

she marveled. "In the days of no air conditioning, they still managed to keep cool by having louvered shutters which could be arranged to keep out the sun and still catch the breeze."

"I suppose you've also learned about the scuppers—also called scuttles—which are like hatch covers on a ship, but in this case release hot air from the attics or upper stories."

Fran blushed at the twinkle in Larry's eyes. "Why didn't you tell me to shut up!" she demanded accusingly.

"Guess I was too busy thinking what a big help you could be to me with all this new-found interest in Conch architecture."

Fran stared at him for several seconds. "Do you mean it, Larry? *Could* I be of help? I think I'd love it, if you wouldn't mind putting up with me."

"Can't think of anything I'd like better than 'putting up' with you, honey. We may find this partnership such a success we'll decide to make it permanent."

"Careful, Larry. I may jump to conclusions and take that for a marriage proposal," Fran teased. Then, when he looked embarrassed, she reached across and squeezed his sturdy hands with both of hers. Too late she noticed he wasn't looking at her at all, but over her shoulder.

"Hope I'm not barging into the middle of a tender scene." The deep, familiar voice, heavily underlined with sarcasm, was so unexpected that Fran jumped visibly, first tightening her grip on Larry's hands, and then pulling away quickly as if she'd been discovered in a guilty act.

Jonathan! How long had he been standing there? Had he heard her foolishness about mistaking Larry's comment as a marriage proposal? The thought made her so uncomfortable she dreaded meeting the gray eyes, invariably lit by a quizzical expression which would give her no clue to his thoughts.

"Say, you should have let us know ahead of time you'd be this early. We'd have waited lunch for you," Larry spoke in the tense silence.

"As usual, I didn't know until the last minute if I'd be able to get away." Jonathan sounded weary, and when he had moved with his quiet tread to sit at one of the extra chairs at the table, Fran dared a quick look at him, and noted the lines of fatigue around his mouth and eyes.

He scraped the chair back from the table far enough to allow his long legs to stretch in front of him. Then, with hands linked behind his head, he groaned and flexed his shoulder muscles.

Fran took the opportunity to study him a little closer, her senses keenly aware of the long muscular hardness of his body. The severe simplicity of his blue business suit only heightened rather than obscured the force of his masculinity. Dark hair showed evidence of his having run impatient fingers through it, and her fingertips tingled oddly at the observation.

With a shock, she realized he had opened his eyes and shifted the position of his head slightly, inspecting her appearance as closely as she was his. While his features had lost some of their tenseness, he had about him the invisible guard that never lowered in her presence.

Conscious of his gaze in a way she never experienced with Larry, she felt exasperation at her own inexplicable behavior. Why could Jonathan just walk into a room and disconcert her the way he did? It was patently ridiculous, but nevertheless her pulses were drumming away in an erratic tempo. She found it necessary to say something to keep from squirming under the impact of those unfathomable eyes.

"Larry offered to let me help him."

"Oh? And in what capacity does Larry require your help?"

Fran gulped in surprise at the steel edge of his tone and looked over to see that Larry appeared as taken aback as she felt.

"Fran has been regaling me over lunch with the architectural lore she's learning at school. She's turning into quite the expert on Conch houses, and it occurred to me she might enjoy putting her knowledge to use."

"And I would!" Fran broke into Larry's explanation, faintly alarmed at the open hostility on Jonathan's face as he regarded his friend through eyes narrowed to gray slits. Why did Jonathan seem so against the idea? He appeared angry at Larry for even suggesting it—or was he upset with *her* for some reason?

Before she could get a clue to his unexpected reaction, his mood changed like quicksilver. "We'll talk about it later. The idea does have possibilities," he said smoothly. "At the moment, I'm too tired to think about anything. But a swim and a brief spell in the sun should cure that."

"I envy you." Larry sighed and stood up, the extra pounds he carried around his waistline evident in the casual beltless slacks and sport shirt he wore. "Me, I've got to talk to some contractors this afternoon."

"Will you be down on Whitehead?"

Larry nodded affirmative and with a smile at Fran started to leave. Unaccountably nervous at the prospect of losing the good-natured buffer of his presence between herself and Jonathan, especially considering the strange way Jonathan was acting, Fran returned his smile with dazzling force. "I'm off this afternoon. Can I go with you?"

Both men spoke in unison.

"Sure."

71

*"NO!"*

All three seemed temporarily frozen into place, stunned into silence. Fran had risen from her chair as she asked the question, confident Larry would not deny her request to accompany him. Jonathan had reacted with the predatory swiftness of a jungle cat as he straightened and reached over to capture her hand, stopping her.

"Fran, I'd like you to stay here with me. We need to talk."

In spite of the conciliatory phrasing, she knew he wasn't requesting her to stay. He was *ordering* her. And he didn't release her hand, but held it gripped tightly in his own. She could feel the tensile strength in those long, shapely fingers. Fascinated, she watched him as he rubbed his thumb across the silver and turquoise ring she wore on her middle finger.

"Well, in that case, I'll leave the two of you to your unearned leisure. Think of me slaving away in this heat." Underneath Larry's jocular manner was puzzlement over what had taken place among them.

When he had gone, Fran felt increasingly awkward standing in front of Jonathan with her hand imprisoned in his. The firm contact with his flesh was doing strange things to her. Every nerve in her body seemed to have raised an alarm, and her heart answered with a pronounced thud against the wall of her ribcage.

She tried without success to pull free of him, avoiding eye contact. Then finally she looked at him, expecting mockery or amusement or perhaps even disapproval, and saw none of it. The gray eyes had dropped their veil and were filled with admiration as they slid over her. "You're beautiful," he murmured in a voice that moved over her like a caress, awakening a strange tremor. She remembered the feel of his lips that long ago night, the only time he had ever kissed her, and the muscular hardness of his body held against hers. The memory was profoundly disturbing.

Immediately upon realizing what she was thinking and feeling, Fran was swept by an inner disgust that her face must have reflected. This time when she pulled away from Jonathan, he released her hand. She could only stand there in front of him, eyes downcast, breasts rising and falling agitatedly as she struggled to compose herself.

"Fran, look at me."

Reluctantly, she raised her eyes to his and saw no emotion there except concern. She might have imagined the powerful desire she'd seen there only seconds earlier.

"I want you to tell me exactly how you felt just now." The eyes and hard jawline were unrelenting as she stared at him with eyes widened first by instinctive protest, and then by shame. She swallowed, accomplishing little in the effort to eliminate the dryness from her throat. There was no impatience in him, but he wasn't to be evaded, either.

"Just now, when I held your hand, was it repugnant to you?"

She shook her head emphatically. "No. I guess I-I liked it at first."

"Then how did you feel?"

"Disgusted with myself." Her hand pressed against her waist as if indicating the exact location of her emotion. Suddenly she was shaking uncontrollably and her hands went up to cover her face as the tears spilled down her cheeks. His arms closed around her, strong and gentle, drawing her against him. She pressed her head against the hard chest, mindless of the damage her tears might do to his white shirt front. He made no attempt to quiet the emotional storm, which ended with surprising quickness, just as it had erupted.

"I don't know what got into me," she mumbled against him, making no effort to free herself. "I never cry."

When he spoke, there was a strange undertone of anger, and the words made little sense to her. "Men like your father ought to be shot." Before she could ask what her father had to do with anything, he had released her and given her a gentle push in the direction of the house. "Now go and put on your swimsuit."

Nearly an hour later, Fran heaved herself up on the edge of the large rectangular pool. "You win!" she gasped, glistening with water like a sleek seal. Anyone seeing her now wouldn't believe she had been devastated by her emotions only a short time ago. In a brief white bikini, she looked like a superb specimen of young womanhood at its healthiest and most beautiful.

Jonathan completed several more laps as if to further impress upon her his superior stamina, and then swam toward her with smooth, powerful strokes. His teeth glinted white against deeply tanned skin as he came up close and treaded water, and Fran knew he was preparing a teasing remark. Without stopping to consider her action, she reached out one foot and pushed his dark head under the water. Before she had time to laugh at the startled expression on his face as he went under, she felt a steel grip around one ankle and she herself tumbled forward into the pool.

Sputtering, she surfaced, only to feel the threatening pressure of a hand on top of her head. "Don't!" she begged, trying to look properly contrite and then giggling in spite of herself. "You looked so f-funny."

"Careful, you're in a very vulnerable position," growled a low warning close beside her, and she treaded water, smiling into his face. Acting on impulse, she reached out and smoothed aside the wet hair plastering his brow. For one breathless moment she watched something flame deep in his eyes and before she knew what was going to happen, he touched his mouth to hers. The kiss was so brief and unexpected, she didn't recoil, and her lips tingled for a long time afterward.

For several minutes there was silence as they both climbed out of the pool and collapsed on lounge chairs a small distance apart. Jonathan lay with his eyes closed, not speaking, and Fran soon concluded he had fallen asleep. She adjusted her own chair slightly so that she could have a better view of his long, still form.

The swimsuit he wore was dark green and fit like a second skin, hugging low on his hips and making no secret of his masculinity. His body was lean, and suggestive of sinewy power, without being too thin. She wondered how he maintained the deep bronze of his tan when he was away so much of the time in the north on business. Or was he? Maybe he relaxed in the sun in vacation places other than Key West? The possibility brought an unpleasant little sensation to her chest.

"Why the frown?"

She started in surprise at the softly spoken question and looked quickly away from him. Had he been looking at her, too, the whole time she was studying him with such undisguised interest. Otherwise, how could he have known she was frowning? The realization embarrassed her.

"Oh, nothing," she lied. "The sun's just bright."

He didn't speak again for several seconds, and some instinct told her he wasn't fooled. Jonathan had the uncanny ability to look into her mind, and the prospect of what he might find there just now was unsettling.

"How's school?"

Welcoming the change of subject, she gave him an account of the classes she was attending. Several times she thought he might have dropped off to sleep, but when she paused in her discourse, he would ask a question or make a comment that let her know he had been listening closely. When he seemed satisfied on the subject of school, he asked, "How are you and Eleanor getting along?"

"Oh, fine. She's good to work for—and very nice to me. Who knows, she may make a silk purse of this sow's ear yet." The flippancy was really a cover-up for the very real sense of inadequacy she sometimes felt in the presence of the older woman, whose shop was patronized by wealthy fashion-conscious women not just from Key West, but from places as far afield as Los Angeles and New York. Eleanor had been written about in some of the foremost women's magazines.

Fran wasn't informed about the background of Jonathan's friendship with Eleanor, but they apparently had known each other a long time, and not just in Key West. Jonathan had, Fran suspected, put Eleanor in charge of both guiding her in the selection of a wardrobe, and tutoring her in the arts of female grooming so foreign to her old life.

"Eleanor is not only a good businesswoman—she's a pretty special human being."

Fran heard the admiration in his voice with a twinge amazingly like jealousy. Was there something more than friendship between him and Eleanor? Lost in her own reflections, Fran let down the back of her lounge chair and flopped over on her stomach, resting one cheek on the cushion of her hands.

All these questions from Jonathan and answers from herself skirted the real issue, as far as she was concerned. Why had he forced her to make such a drastic change in her life? People didn't do things for no reason, and she just couldn't figure out his motivation. Even though she had grown accustomed to luxury so quickly it amazed her, she still felt odd knowing she was living in Jonathan's house and eating at his table, driving a car nobody except her used and not paying him a cent in return. She didn't even lift a finger in running his household.

How well she remembered the day he'd taken her outside, where a shiny blue Triumph convertible was parked in the driveway, and told her it was hers to use. "But I can't drive!" she'd protested.

"You can learn. Everyone needs to drive an automobile, and you'll have transportation to and from work and school." As usual Jonathan was implacable in his decision. At the time, she had declared she could ride her bicycle as she had always done, but then she took the job working for Eleanor, and began to wear high-heeled shoes and chic outfits that were anything but cycling attire.

The burden of indebtedness to him weighed heavily during moments like this one. If only there was something she could do to repay him in some measure, she could salve her conscience. Had Larry been serious about her being able to help him with the restoration work? The idea appealed strongly.

She lifted her head. "Jonathan?" He seemed deeply engrossed in thoughts that must be somber, judging from the severity of his expression. Somehow she didn't think he was really seeing the lushness of tropical shrubbery maintained so beautifully by Joseph. When the gray eyes swung to meet hers, she was disturbed by the dark emotion in them, and spoke quickly.

"What do you think of Larry's suggestion that I work with him on the houses?"

Irritation flashed across his features, but was brought quickly under control. "You and Larry seem to get on very well."

"We do!" she assured eagerly. "He makes me feel good about myself," she explained sincerely, and then wondered at the black look Jonathan leveled at her. A surge of anger removed the reticence she frequently felt in his presence. "I don't know why you looked at me like that just now. I have to have *some* friends, don't I? And Larry's a nice person. Besides—I'd like to do something to pay you back." Her indignation faded to wistfulness as she gave him the last and most important reason.

He was quiet for several moments. "I think you may find working with Larry very beneficial," he said finally, his thoughtful tone causing her to regret her own recent vehemence.

"I can't wait to tell Larry!" she said excitedly, sitting up on the edge of her lounge chair. Jonathan seemed impervious to the smile she beamed upon him.

"You can go with me in a little while and tell him the glad tidings," he said shortly. "But first there are two things I want to make perfectly clear. Number One, Larry is in grave danger at this time of falling in love with you—if he hasn't already. Number Two, you're under my control until the end of the year, and you're not marrying anybody during that time."

Fran stared at him, too amazed to speak. Whatever she had expected to hear from him, it was neither of these two astounding pronouncements. She blurted words that surprised her almost as much as his: "Why shouldn't Larry fall in love with me?"

A savage expression crossed his features and was replaced by a quizzical half smile that cloaked his thoughts. With a fluid movement he rose to his feet, towering over her. "No reason at all you would understand, my innocent. Come along and get dressed."

Fran obeyed, oddly disappointed at his answer.

They rode in silence the short distance to the house on Whitehead Street where Larry was in consultation with the head contractor hired to oversee all the construction work. Both men were perspiring, their clothing clinging to their moist bodies, and they looked rather enviously at Jonathan and Fran, who showed every evidence of having recently stepped from the shower.

Larry's eyes lingered on Fran as he performed the introductions. She smiled back at him and announced, "Jonathan says I can work with you—if it's all right with you."

She heard something resembling a snort from the tall man beside her, but kept her attention on Larry, who beamed his assurance that it was definitely "all right" with him, as she had been sure it would be. The contractor observed the three of them with restrained curiosity, but kept his own counsel.

Fran was soon engrossed in the discussion of plans for this initial restoration project. Mindless of the earlier tension between herself and Jonathan and the afternoon heat and dust swirling the air, she trooped through the old house with the three men and listened avidly to their conversation. Larry was thoroughly professional as he evaluated the extent of the work to be done. "The underframes in this old house were ground pinned, which means they're attached to cedar posts driven all the way to bedrock. So the foundation is sound."

She found it all quite fascinating and was surprised when they emerged from the house to find that hours had passed. Later when she had returned to Garrett House and was changing clothes for the third time that day, she realized she felt more than a little like some kind of Cinderella living in the glamorous ambiance of the ball. Just remember, she reminded herself, at the end of this year you'll have to go back to reality.

Sometimes she forgot that this living arrangement with Jonathan was only temporary, and at the end of the stipulated time he would owe her nothing. She probably wouldn't even see him again after that. The possibility brought such dismay that she resolutely banished the line of thought and concentrated on dressing for dinner.

She was struggling with the zipper of a sleeveless white dress with a scooped neckline when there was a knock at her bedroom door. She'd chosen the dress because the soft silk jersey fabric felt deliciously cool against her skin, clinging in all the right places and emphasizing the golden brown of her tan.

"Come in," she called automatically, tugging desperately at the zipper. With luck, that might be Joanna or Maria, either of whom could give her a hand. But it was neither. Jonathan stood in the open doorway surveying her difficulty as her hands increased their frenzied efforts to deal with the recalcitrant zipper.

"Turn around," he ordered, striding across the room toward her. Her pulses quickened madly at his nearness and without speaking she obeyed him. His warm breath brushed against her bare flesh and set off a complex reaction all along her spine as he bent and worked with the zipper until he had pulled it free of the obstructing material and then slid it firmly up her back. The touch of his fingers had caused ripples of sensation, and she gave an involuntary shiver as she turned and faced him.

"Thank you," she said nervously, hoping he hadn't noticed the shiver or realized how his nearness affected her.

"Any time." A rueful little smile softened the sternness of his handsome features as he stood there looking disturbingly masculine in a lightweight suit superbly tailored to his lean physique.

"I have something for you," he said, reaching into a pocket and bringing out a small jeweler's box. Nonplussed, Fran stared at it while he flipped open the tiny lid and took a ring from the satin bed. Before she could speak or move, he had taken her hand, removed her silver and turquoise ring, and slid the ring from the box onto her finger.

"Do you like it?" He watched her as she held out her hand and stared entranced at the large square stone flanked on two sides by diamonds. Did she *like* it! It was breathtakingly beautiful—of course, she *more* than liked it; even she could tell the stone was a sapphire, which meant the ring must have cost an enormous amount of money.

"It's beautiful," she murmured, turning her hand this way and that to catch the play of light on the facets of the exquisite stones. Her eyes were huge blue pools of questioning as she looked up at him. Why had he bought something like this for her? The expression on her face was gravely thoughtful as she asked hesitantly, "Jonathan—how do you explain me to your friends?"

He lifted his shoulders in a noncommittal shrug, but didn't try to pretend he didn't understand what she was asking. "Up to now, I haven't been in Key West enough to feel the need to 'explain' you. But you're right. There will inevitably be questions as to our relationship. Any suggestions?"

She gazed up into his face, momentarily at a loss as to how to reply. Her knees suddenly threatened to buckle under her at any instant, and she moved over to perch on the bench in front of the vanity.

"Maybe you could say I'm related to you in some way. A distant cousin or something who you just happened to run into here in Key West."

He appeared to be turning the suggestion over in his mind, presumably considering its merits and deficiencies. "Sounds a little flimsy, don't you think? I think I might have a more . . . *credible* explanation for your presence in my house."

The way he was looking directly into her eyes took her breath away. "Wh-what do you have in m-mind?" She sounded as disconcerted as she felt.

His eyes flicked down to the sapphire and diamond ring. "I could introduce you as my fiancée."

Fran leaped to her feet, staring at him as if he had just given conclusive proof of having escaped from a mental institution. "That's the *craziest* thing I ever heard of! *Nobody* would believe that you—I—that we . . ." She couldn't even complete the objection to a suggestion too preposterous for words.

"Oh, no?" His short laugh was sardonic. "Convincing Key West society that you and I are engaged will be no problem, believe me. Especially with the male contingent."

"Do you really *want* to—to tell people that?" She was still stunned with the initial shock of his suggestion and grappling with the notion that he might be willing to have people in his own social class think he was engaged to *her*. It was incredible.

"An engagement does seem the all-around solution to more than one problem," he answered enigmatically. "We can start by breaking the news to Larry tonight."

"Oh, no!"

He looked forbidding at her outburst, his eyebrows raised in arrogant questioning. "Why not, may I ask?"

"Larry's your friend—and mine, too, I think. Don't you think he should know the truth?"

"The truth as far as the world, *including* Larry, is concerned is that you have accepted my proposal of marriage. Nobody need be told any different."

Her will was no match for his. Her troubled gaze lowered before the penetration of his and once again she submitted to the inflexibility of his judgment. She understood this unfathomable man no better now than she ever had, but she was completely under his domination.

And how could she refuse to agree to this seemingly innocent deception in view of his unstinting generosity toward her? It was asking so little of her to pretend to be engaged to him, and he apparently thought the imposture would be of benefit in forestalling idle gossip. She had no choice—she would do what Jonathan asked of her.

# Chapter Six

Larry was obviously unprepared for the announcement of Fran's engagement to Jonathan. His face went dull red, and for a second or two the kindly brown eyes regarded her with the hurt expression of a faithful dog who has been administered an unexpected and undeserved kick.

She longed to deny the falsehood Jonathan was erecting with such coolness, to cry out, "It isn't really true, Larry!" She felt awful deceiving him like this when he'd been her mainstay during the past difficult weeks. His hurt and disappointment were distressingly evident in the brief span of time before he covered his emotions and gave them his congratulations in a stiffly reticent manner.

Later in the evening she remembered what Jonathan had said by the pool that afternoon, that Larry was in danger of falling in love with her. Amazing as the idea had been to her at the time, she wondered now if there weren't some truth in it. Something in Larry's demeanor hinted of reproach, as if she had betrayed him.

But if it were true that Larry's affection for her went beyond that of a friend, how had Jonathan known? The idea of someone like Larry—or Jonathan—falling in love with her just wouldn't have occurred to her. Not that she suffered from a terrible inferiority complex. She would have had to be both blind and stupid not to recognize her physical attractiveness to men. But she also knew she belonged to a world apart from the one in which Larry and Jonathan moved with such ease. Both of them had been born to wealth, educated in some of the best schools the country had to offer and were widely traveled. They were out of her sphere.

She needed to keep reminding herself that the last three months were just some incredible interlude in her life. It would have to end—the question was, when? Her presence at the dinner table with these two highly successful men, she beautifully dressed in an expensive gown and wearing a magnificent sapphire ring on her left hand: this was the stuff of fairy tales, material for the most unrealistic brand of fiction.

"When do you plan to make a formal announcement of your—uh, engagement?" Larry's stilted question brought her back to the present. The conversation had been concentrated on the restoration work when her thoughts drifted off on their own course. Her eyes flashed automatically to Jonathan, who appeared not the least perturbed.

"Personally, I'd prefer to hear all the *oohs* and *ahs* at one time and get it over with. Eleanor's party this weekend should provide the perfect opportunity. I suspect she's invited everybody on the island who's likely to be even tepidly interested in our big news."

Fran's heartbeat accelerated with fright. She hadn't even known of the party until now. So far she had not met socially with Jonathan's friends and acquaintances in Key West. The prospect of being inspected by them under any circumstances was daunting enough, but to have to stand up before all of them as Jonathan's fiancée! She couldn't do it!

Her eyes must have reflected her panic because Jonathan quickly changed the subject with news of a former classmate of his and Larry's who had just been elected to a judgeship in the state where he was practicing law. She was grateful for the opportunity to sit quietly and try to calm the apprehension knotting her insides.

By the time Larry excused himself, declaring with strained jocularity his intentions of getting to bed early to restore himself for the trials of the morrow, Fran had steeled her resolve to have a serious talk with Jonathan and convince him how farfetched this whole engagement idea was.

After dinner, as had become their custom, the three had been sitting on the brick patio, the two men indulging their preference for coffee and brandy following the evening meal. When Larry had gone, Fran got up restlessly from her chair and walked a few steps to the lovely little fountain in the middle of the patio, its steady flow of water dropping from the cupped hands of a white marble nymph into the circular pool. With shoulders slightly hunched and arms folded tensely against her midriff, Fran summoned her courage to speak.

"Cold?"

The deep, solicitous voice startled her with its nearness, and she jumped slightly. Then before she could muster an answer through her constricted throat, strong arms came around her and pulled her close.

The shiver had nothing to do with the temperature of the air as she closed her eyes for a brief moment and leaned back against him, allowing the sensation of warmth and security to creep through her. She breathed in the clean, masculine smell of him, a tantalizing combination of soap, aftershave lotion and male flesh. Her relaxation was short-lived, though. His lips brushed against the side of her neck finding an incredibly sensitive area below her ear and stimulating an immediate and alarming reaction from her body.

Her breasts seemed to grow heavier and the nipples hardened against the silky white bodice. She felt unaccountably weak, as if all the rigid tissue of her bones had gone to mush; and a small, insistent ache in her lower torso attested to a passion that had lain dormant until now. Her breathing was suddenly shallow and rapid.

"Jonathan," she said weakly.

At the sound of her voice, he lifted his head from her neck and shoulders, allowing her some relief in the devastation of her senses, but he still held her firmly against him.

"What, Fran?" It seemed she could feel as well as hear the huskiness of his voice.

"I can't go through this engagement thing. I can't face all those people at Eleanor's."

"You're going to have to be a little more convincing than you were with Larry tonight."

How could he sound so matter-of-fact when she felt anything but calm. Couldn't he feel her heart pounding against the steel of his arm curving under her breasts?

"Fran, do you trust me?"

The softly spoken question took her aback with its unexpectedness. Her mind grappled with it as efficiently as was possible in her present position of being held disconcertingly against his hard length.

"Why, yes, I suppose so," she said finally.

He turned her around to face him, and she could see the humorous slant of his mouth. "Not exactly a rousing avowal of confidence, but better than nothing, I suppose." He held her lightly by the waist, giving her the choice of gazing at his white shirt front or tipping back her head in order to see his face. She chose the latter.

"If you trust me, you have to believe I wouldn't ask you to do anything beyond your capabilities *or* detrimental to your well-being. You *will* be able to face the people at Eleanor's party, and they'll be charmed by you. They're nice people, not ogres. And I'll be right beside you the whole time."

From his careful wording and reasoning manner, he might have been allaying the fears of a child, but Fran couldn't find it in her to take offense. The gentleness of his voice was like a soft caress easing the tension of her spirit.

"I guess I can try," she murmured uncertainly. How could she hope to resist his will when he stood so close that his masculinity was a tangible force assaulting her senses, holding her captive.

"One thing you're going to have to work on, though, if we intend to convince anyone our engagement is real. You can't freeze up every time I touch you."

"I can't help it." She regretted the impulsive rejoinder as soon as it escaped her mouth when she saw Jonathan's features harden and heard the icy distance in his voice, which had been so warm and gentle seconds earlier.

"You don't seem to react that way to physical contact with Larry." His gray eyes bored into her apologetic ones, demanding an answer.

"It—it's not the same. . . . I don't *feel* anything when Larry touches me."

He didn't say anything for what seemed to her heightened perceptions a long time. When he did speak, the hoarse undertone in his voice increased her sharp awareness of the strange power he exerted over her senses. "The only solution is for you to become accustomed to my touching you. Just relax and trust me."

She stood absolutely still as he framed her face in both his hands and slowly lowered his lips toward hers. She didn't move or try to resist when he just barely placed his mouth on her own, teasingly so that she involuntarily lifted her head a little to make the contact firmer. Then he moved his mouth tenderly against hers as if savoring the sweet softness. All Fran's deepest instincts bade her to slip her arms up around his neck and pull him down closer to her, but before she knew what was happening, he had lifted his head away from her and released her. She experienced a crushing wave of disappointment that went quite beyond her understanding. Didn't Jonathan *like* kissing her?

"So here you are, Jonathan! I had to fight my way through two female bodyguards to get to you."

The womanly voice was like ice-cold water, awakening Fran from a world of trance to reality. Framed in the mellow lighting of the patio was the same beautiful blonde Fran had already seen on two previous occasions. Both times she had given clear indication of her intimacy with Jonathan. Tonight, she wore a calf-length black dress that emphasized every curve of her shapely figure.

Dismissing Fran with a single indifferent glance, she held out both hands toward Jonathan. "Darling, why do you look so surprised to see me? I told you last week I couldn't wait to get away from the social whirl for a few weeks and just vegetate in the sun for awhile. And what better place to vegetate than Key West? Of course, if I'm intruding, I'll just take a taxi back to the Casa Marina. . . ." Her full red lips pouted provocatively.

Jonathan recovered from the unexpectedness of his

lovely guest's arrival and moved over as if to take the hands extended demandingly toward him. But when he came close, she slipped her arms around his neck and pressed her lips against his in a long kiss.

Fran's reaction shook her with its violence. At first, the woman's words had pelted her spirit with the brittle hardness of hailstones. And now it seemed she was expected to stand over to one side, forgotten, while Jonathan made love to the woman right in front of her. Perhaps what shocked Fran about her reaction more than anything else was her unwillingness to make a quiet exit and leave the two of them alone together. She had no intention of being ignored this way.

"Jonathan, you haven't introduced me to your *friend.*"

Immediately she regretted the boldness of her impulse to draw their attention, as well as the asperity of her tone. The sleek blonde drew back a little to regard Fran with the same annoyance she might have bestowed upon a pesky insect, and Jonathan's expression was unfathomable.

"Forgive my bad manners," he said smoothly. "I didn't remember that you two haven't officially met. Fran Bright and Anne Taylor. Now why don't we sit down out here. Can I get either of you something to drink?"

"I'll have the usual, darling," Anne purred, giving him a confidential smile that relegated Fran to the role of outsider.

"One dry martini coming up. Would you like something, Fran? Orange juice?" Jonathan didn't seem to notice the open derision on the face of Anne Taylor as he made this recommendation.

"Make me a manhattan, *darling.*"

Blue eyes wide with incredulity at her own boldness met gray eyes narrowed in swift reaction to her perfect imitation of the other woman's sugary endearment. Jonathan hesitated as if he meant to say something, then apparently changed his mind. With a courteous inclination of his dark head and an "Excuse me a minute, ladies," he disappeared into the house.

Fran didn't know what had prompted her to ask for a cocktail when she didn't drink. No wonder Jonathan had looked at her so strangely. For one uneasy moment, she'd thought he was going to show her up in front of the sophisticated Anne by refusing to serve her an alcoholic drink.

Now that he was gone, Anne Taylor didn't waste any time in interrogating Fran, her intentions immediately clear. "What do you, ah, *do*—Fran, wasn't it?"

Fran plunged in with the immediate sensation that she was way over her head. "I work, I go to school and I'm also helping Larry Bingham with the restoration of some old houses Jonathan owns here in Key West." Her tone said she was a very busy person.

"I see."

The workings of Anne's mind weren't difficult for Fran to read. The blonde was wondering just what Fran's relationship with Jonathan was.

"Are you studying architecture, then?"

"No, I'm just taking general courses like history and English." Some perversity led Fran to reveal more than was necessary without satisfying the other woman's curiosity.

"How did you happen to meet Jonathan?" Puzzlement lurked in the icy blue depths as Anne tried to chase down an elusive memory.

"We just kind of ran into each other, you might say." Unconsciously, Fran adopted an air of cool sophistication totally uncharacteristic of her. She was playing a role, and she hadn't the faintest idea why she was doing it.

"What do *you* do?" The subtle impudence in the question brought an angry gleam to the other woman's eyes.

"I can't wait to hear the answer to that question, Anne. What *do* you do?" The undertone of amusement in Jonathan's voice as he rejoined them carrying a tray of drinks betrayed his awareness of the thinly veiled antagonism which had developed between the two women during his absence.

"Jonathan," Anne reproved sulkily, "you know I spend lots of time doing volunteer work. Why should I put time and work into a career when I don't *need* to earn an income. I'd only be taking a position away from somebody who really needs it." Her blue eyes flicked meaningfully to Fran, having found an obvious example of someone who "needed" to work.

Jonathan busied himself placing a low table within easy reach and handing each of them their drink. Fran eyed the amber liquid in hers and resisted the impulse to eat the maraschino cherry, knowing it wouldn't fit her role of sophisticated woman of the world.

"Here, darling, sit next to me."

Jonathan sat in the chair Anne had indicated, but only after moving it so that he was positioned between the two of them. "You ladies seem to have broken the ice while I was gone," he offered blandly.

Fran avoided meeting his eyes, raising her drink to her lips. In her nervousness, she took a healthy gulp and then nearly choked as the fiery liquid burned her throat.

"Is your drink all right?" Jonathan inquired, a strong note of irony underlying the more obvious concern in his voice.

"Perfect," she managed to get out, favoring him with a dazzling smile of reassurance.

Anne had observed this brief exchange with sharp

interest, a tiny frown wrinkling the smooth perfection of her brow. "Jonathan," she said slowly, looking from one to the other, "why did you say earlier that Fran and I hadn't *officially* met? She does look terribly familiar and yet I can't remember when . . ." Suddenly she inhaled audibly and sat bolt upright in the deeply cushioned chair which encouraged one to lounge.

"The singer! The one in those ghastly clothes we saw that day collecting money from the tourists!" Her voice exuded distaste at the memory, but something forbidding in Jonathan's expression quickly stopped her from continuing in that vein. "You are the same girl?" she asked in a more restrained voice.

Under totally different circumstances, Fran might have been humiliated by the other woman's outburst. But she had downed the contents of her glass, forcing herself to take gulps of the nasty bittersweet cocktail, and already she was feeling the effects of the alcohol. Her head felt strangely light and she was much warmer than the temperature of the evening air warranted, but she was no longer in the least intimidated by either of her two companions.

"As a matter of fact, I am," she replied calmly, aware of Jonathan's intent gaze. She looked archly at him and produced another specimen of what she intended to be a devastating smile. "Can I have another drink, Jonathan? How about you, Anne?"

Though clearly affronted by Fran's blatant assumption of the role of hostess in Jonathan's house, Anne contented herself with draining the contents of her glass and then handing it to him. "Thank you, darling. I guess I have to keep up with the competition."

"Which in this particular case should be interesting," Jonathan drawled enigmatically and once again left them together.

Now the barriers of politeness were down. "Don't

you think you're a little *young* for a man Jonathan's age?" Sarcasm curled Anne's lips, spoiling the classical beauty of her features.

"I don't think so," Fran replied loftily. "Jonathan must not think so, either." She held up her hand and studied the sapphire and diamond ring, which up until that moment she had forgotten. "Did you notice what Jonathan gave me?"

Without waiting for an answer, she leaned forward and held out her hand to give Anne a full view. "Of course, it's not the traditional engagement ring, but I love it."

Anne gasped. "Why, you little fool! You don't for one moment actually believe Jonathan would *marry* the likes of you!"

"We plan to make a formal announcement at Eleanor's party this weekend. I suppose you're acquainted with her?" Heady with the sense of her own power, Fran watched the other woman's struggle for self-control and had to admire her, if grudgingly, for her victory. She looked up as Jonathan emerged from the house with more drinks.

"Fran's been telling me the most incredible story, darling—that you and she are *engaged*." The intonation and accompanying laugh emphasized just how ridiculous she considered the idea.

"The only thing incredible about it is my good luck. I am surprised to hear Fran has confided in you. She was so reluctant earlier this evening to make our good news public." Jonathan set Fran's drink on the table in front of her and then stood behind her, one hand dropping to caress her bare neck and shoulder, the light contact igniting flames of sensation that licked along her veins right to her fingertips and toes.

She leaned forward to pick up her drink and was both relieved and disappointed when he moved to take his own chair. Anne was regarding both of them with a mixture of hostility and disbelief. "Something's going on here. I'm just not sure what it is," she said suspiciously.

"Every bachelor, no matter how stalwart, has to go down sooner or later," Jonathan declared lightly, watching Fran tilt her glass and gulp the contents, which were still nasty but didn't burn her throat as much as at first. "If you're planning to be around this weekend, Eleanor's giving one of her garden soirees. Should be worth going to, if you've got nothing better to do."

"I'm surprised your fiancée allows you to keep up your friendship with an old flame." Anne's tone was insinuating and her glance toward Fran malicious.

The barb hit target. From the first Fran had wondered if there existed an intimate relationship between Eleanor and Jonathan, and here was everything but actual proof of it. The thought made her dizzy. Or at least *something* made her dizzy. She was beginning to experience great difficulty concentrating on the conversation. Draining her glass, she set it carefully on the table and was amazed to learn how poorly she had calculated the distance, glass banging sharply against glass.

Suddenly she wanted nothing more than to make a dignified exit and go straight to her room. It seemed a simple enough ambition, but was something of a problem in the execution.

"If you two will excuse me . . ." she mumbled and stood up, only to be alarmed at the way everything around her was unfocused and wavering, like objects under water. Jonathan moved with amazing swiftness and supported her around the waist with one arm. She heard Anne's voice from far away. "I suppose you'll have to drive your little waif home," and then Jonathan at his most forbidding, "She *is* home."

Her legs kept buckling under her in the most embarrassing way as she walked beside him across the rough bricks of the patio, her feet repeatedly catching on their edges. Without the support of that steel band around her waist, she would never have made it to the door. Once inside and away from Anne's watchful eyes, Jonathan abandoned all pretense of helping her walk under her own power and scooped her up into his arms.

"You little idiot," he muttered under his breath.

Overwhelmed by the urgent need to apologize to him for her appalling behavior with Anne, she clutched him with both arms and pressed her face into his neck. "I'm sorry, Jonathan," she mumbled thickly, and kissed him awkwardly.

She felt a tremor pass through his body and interpreted it as evidence of his irritation, but he didn't say anything as he carried her up the stairs and into her bedroom. He laid her across the bed, ordering, "Turn over." With his help she obeyed, not stopping to question the command. Then she felt the vibration of the zipper moving down her back and realized he was undressing her.

"'S okay," she mumbled, meaning to assure him she could manage the rest by herself. But he was turning her over and easing the dress down over her arms and then tugging it free of her hips. She felt powerless to cooperate or resist. He sat on the edge of the bed, holding her up against him while he unhooked her bra, a flimsy creation of nylon and lace.

Before undressing her any further, he cradled her against him, stroking her back, completely bare now, with hands that trembled. His heart thudded violently in his chest—she knew because she could feel the jarring vibration against her bare breasts.

"Jonathan—" She tried desperately to make something coherent of her confused thoughts and feelings, but failed miserably, ending with a deep sigh of frustration. Then she felt herself laid gently between the smooth sheets, and knew fleetingly that she was naked before his eyes but didn't feel ashamed.

When he had tucked the top sheet securely under her arms, he bent down and kissed her on the lips. Her arms came up around his neck the way they'd wanted to do earlier that evening on the patio before Anne interrupted.

"Don't go yet," she heard herself say, hoping she could explain how sorry she was to have embarrassed him in front of his friend.

There was a low, husky laugh. "Out of the mouths of babes," came the familiar, ironic voice, and then he was gone.

Her dreams were chaotic. She was involved in tempestuous arguments with Anne Taylor one moment and in the next found herself singing with a band at the Black Pig. Out in the audience were angry faces, including those of Jonathan and Larry. Without any transition, she was wandering through an empty old house trying to find her way to the outside. What she wanted more than anything else was to make her way to the ocean so that she could go swimming. She was dying of thirst!

"What's wrong, darling?" Someone was pulling the sheet back up from the bottom of the bed where she had kicked it in her restless tossing. Cool hands smoothed her hair back from her heated face.

"I'm so thirsty," she complained, coming half awake and recognizing Jonathan sitting on the edge of her bed. What was he doing there?

"It's the booze," he said and disappeared into the bathroom, coming back almost immediately with a paper cup of water. She sat up gratefully, unconscious of the sheet dropping to her waist, and took the cup from him, drinking its contents down greedily. Then she sank back down against the pillow and drifted off to sleep again, oblivious to the presence of the man sitting at the side of the bed.

The next morning she awoke to the buzz of her alarm clock and turned it off with a groan, feeling tired and drained. Memories of the previous evening flooded over her, and she huddled under the sheet, wishing she could remain in the safety of her bed forever and never have to face Anne Taylor *or* Jonathan again. It was all too humiliating to bear! Detail by painful detail, she relived the scene on the patio.

The door opened and Maria stood on the threshold with a tray. Startled, Fran eyed the pitcher of orange juice with longing. Her mouth felt awful, dry and shrunken.

"Mr. Talbot said to bring this up to you," Maria explained with her usual deadpan expression, and left the tray on the bedside table before departing without a further word.

Fran sat up, clutching her head as a pain shot through it. The sheet had fallen away and she looked down to note that she was wearing not a stitch of clothing, not even her underwear. She vaguely recalled Jonathan carrying her up the stairs. Pressing both hands against her hot cheeks, she realized he must have undressed her. Now she *knew* she'd never be able to look him in the eyes again.

Her head felt as if it weighed a ton as she sat propped up in bed against the pillows, drinking the ice-cold orange juice. Surely nothing had ever tasted better. By the time she had gulped down two full glasses, she felt brave enough to venture getting out of bed. "Oh," she groaned aloud, clutching her throbbing head. Why did people drink that foul tasting alcohol if it made them feel like this the next day?

Moving very carefully over to a narrow oak chest of

drawers, she decided that what she needed was to clear the heaviness from her body with some vigorous exercise. Opening a drawer, she pulled out the first swimsuit her hand encountered, which just happened to be a bright red and white striped bikini. She couldn't remember ever before having to concentrate so hard to fasten a simple hook and tie strings around her neck, but finally she was ready to brave the stairs.

Ordinarily she would have worn a shirt or beach robe over her swimming attire, but today it was too much of an effort to contemplate. Trailing a red terrycloth robe in one hand, she slowly descended the stairs in her bare feet and went through the house and out onto the patio, where she paused, relieved but not surprised to observe that the pool area was deserted. It was still very early. In her present condition, she preferred not to see Larry or Jonathan. Actually she didn't want to see Jonathan ever again, not after last night.

Sitting down gingerly at the edge of the pool, she dangled her feet in the cool water and then slowly lowered her whole body in. Ah, it felt incredibly refreshing! So clean and cool. Ignoring the throbbing ache in her head, she began to swim laps and persevered until she felt like a rock that would soon just sink to the bottom of the pool. Her arms and legs refusing to propel her any farther, she rolled over on her back and floated, shutting her eyes against the cruel early morning glare.

Lulled by the quiet into feeling she was alone in the world, Fran was so startled by the loud impact of a body hitting the pool's surface that she forgot where she was and tried to sit up, sinking under the water instead. Coming back to the surface with a coughing sputter, she saw Jonathan swimming the length of the pool with long, even strokes, and felt panic at the prospect of facing him once he had tired.

Without hesitating, she moved toward the edge of the pool, following a powerful impulse to escape before he might try to stop her. But once she had reached it, she didn't have the energy to swing herself out as she normally would. Instead she clung to the tiled edge, breathing deeply and waiting for the dizziness to subside.

"Feeling a little rough this morning?"

The low voice was right behind her. Jonathan was so close she could feel his bare, wet shoulder against her own. She turned her head and eased her eyes open just wide enough to see him. His teeth were white against the bronze of his face and his gray eyes were kindled with teasing laughter. In place of the disapproval she somehow both expected and dreaded, she saw what looked like good-natured sympathy in his countenance.

"Why did you make me those drinks last night?" she asked dully.

"How could I refuse without making a scene in front of Anne?"

She closed her eyes again, defeated by the truth of his reply. Shame burned inside her at the memory of how she'd held forth like the true sophisticate with Anne Taylor. What on earth had gotten into her to act like that?

"I must have made an awful fool of myself!" she moaned in a low, miserable voice.

"Oh, I wouldn't say that. In some ways I prefer you drunk," he said cheerfully, swinging himself with ease up on the edge of the pool. Before she guessed his intention, he had reached down, grasped her firmly by the upper arms and lifted her up beside him.

Whatever did he mean about preferring her drunk? What an insulting thing to say! "I think drunk people are disgusting," she pronounced stiffly, summoning all the dignity she could manage under the circumstances.

If only she could remember what she'd said and done after leaving the patio last night. It was all somewhat of a blur.

"Sometimes," he said agreeably. "I didn't find that true in your case, although you were considerably friendlier than usual."

Forgetting that abrupt movements caused knifelike pains in her head, Fran turned sharply and stared at him with wide, questioning eyes. Suddenly she remembered waking up naked under the sheet that morning. What had she said to him? What had she *done?*

He threw back his head and laughed at the alarm on her face. "Don't worry. Your virtue is still intact. When I ravish you, you'll remember it."

His lighthearted mood was both reassuring and, inexplicably, provoking. Something tugged at her consciousness, and Fran remembered that Anne Taylor had still been there when she had made her unsteady exit. How long had Anne stayed? Had Jonathan taken her back to the hotel? Did he spend the night with her? Was that the reason behind this early-morning buoyancy? The last conjecture did nothing to lift her heavy spirits.

"I hope I didn't embarrass you last night in front of your girlfriend," she said ill-naturedly.

But that only served to further amuse him. "I hope you aren't going to be one of those jealous, demanding wives."

The amusement in his low voice irked her. "Hardly," she snapped irritably, scrambling to her feet and putting a few feet between them. "I'm not going to be your wife at all." Her headache was forgotten in the urgency to get away from him before she physically attacked him. As she fled toward the house, his laughter sounded in her ears. What was so *funny,* anyway!

After a cool shower, Fran felt considerably better.

She dressed in a dainty white batiste blouse and a simple flared skirt, the crisp color of blue Wedgewood china. Following a light breakfast, she departed for work at the shop.

When she entered it a few minutes later, she found Eleanor lounging comfortably on a low loveseat upholstered in white velvet. She motioned for Fran to sit opposite her. "Coffee?" As usual, the older woman had both hands employed with her inevitable cigarette and black coffee.

"No, thanks. I've already had some," Fran refused, taking the place indicated. A customer came out of a fitting room, and Eleanor's attention shifted to her. While the two women discussed the fit of the slacks suit the woman was trying on, Fran took the opportunity to study Eleanor at close range. What was the term Anne Taylor had used to describe her? Jonathan's "old flame"?

She was extremely tall, at least five feet nine inches or maybe even taller, without the additional height her shoes added, and thin almost to the point of emaciation. Her thick black hair was styled very short and was liberally sprinkled with gray hairs she made no attempt to hide with the use of dye. Her makeup was expertly applied, and her taste in clothes ran to the dramatic.

Fran recognized that Eleanor was a woman no man could ignore. Not only did she dress with flair, but she was poised and witty and too secure in her own worth ever to be petty. Clever, successful, indisputably a woman of the world, Eleanor would make any man proud to have her as his hostess when he entertained.

What was the relationship between her and Jonathan? What had he explained to her about Fran? These were the questions which occupied Fran's mind as she rose to wait on a new arrival. After that she was busy until lunchtime, when there was a lull that gave her the opportunity she had been waiting for to browse through the racks.

"Well, what do you have in mind?" Eleanor's voice, faintly tinged with amusement, made Fran aware that she had been conducting her search with unusual intensity.

"Something special for your party this weekend." Fran had blurted out the truth before it occurred to her to wonder if Eleanor even knew Jonathan intended to bring her. A quick look revealed that the announcement had produced no noticeable effect upon the older woman.

"Any ideas?" Eleanor was every inch the smooth professional, eliciting clues from the undecided customer.

Fran hesitated. "Something to make me look older." She concentrated all her attention on a severely plain black dress she was examining, not daring to look at Eleanor for fear she would see mockery on that sophisticated face.

"How about something really *sexy?*"

The blithe question brought a deep flush to Fran's cheeks, spoiling any attempt she might have made to be offhand. Fortunately, Eleanor didn't even seem to be aware of Fran's discomfiture as she strode purposefully across the deeply carpeted room.

"This will be *perfect* on you! It may not look like much on the hanger, but on your figure it will be absolutely stunning. Especially with your coloring." She laughed at the dubiousness of Fran's expression as she stared at the garment Eleanor held up by one hand.

She was right about at least one thing, Fran reflected to herself. The dress, one of Eleanor's own designs, didn't look like much on the hanger, nor was there much to it. If anything, it looked like a plain satin underslip with tiny rope straps. The color was a pale bronze which shimmered in the subdued lighting of the shop.

"Try it on," Eleanor insisted. Then with a throaty laugh, "You'll have to leave off the bra."

When Fran emerged from the dressing room a few moments later, she felt ridiculously naked before the other woman's frank scrutiny.

"Stunning. Absolutely stunning," Eleanor murmured approvingly.

Fran surveyed herself in full-length triple mirrors. The lustrous satin fabric gleamed with the slightest movement and turn of her body. The plain fitted bodice hugged the firm curves of her breasts. The skirt, narrow and pencil-slim, curved over her narrow hips before falling straight to her ankles. On either side were slits that came up to mid-thigh.

It was an unbelievably bold, seductive dress which required a perfect figure underneath. Fran couldn't believe *she* was the provocative image in the mirror.

"I don't know if I *dare* turn you loose on my male guests in that dress," Eleanor said with mock seriousness. "The understated color brings out your gorgeous tan and shows off your hair color and eyes. It's *your* dress, honey."

"I'll take it," Fran said breathlessly before she could change her mind. She knew it was shockingly expensive and would ruin her week's pay even with the discount.

That evening, to her immense relief, everything seemed to have returned to normal between herself and Larry, as if the engagement announcement had never occurred to interfere with their friendship. Shyness in Jonathan's company prompted her to give the bulk of her attention to Larry, who was much the safer of the two men as far as she was concerned.

Only at one point during the evening was she denied the protection of Larry's company when he excused himself to take a long distance telephone call in the library. She looked up to find Jonathan's eyes on her and lowered her own quickly before the knowing expression in his. He knew that he disconcerted her! He seemed to know everything about the way she felt.

"How do you feel?" he asked, reminding her of the previous evening and her unprecedented behavior under the influence of alcohol.

"Oh—everything's back to normal," she replied nonchalantly.

"I was afraid of that."

At a loss as to what to say in response to that enigmatic comment, she searched for a safe topic. "I got a letter from Aunt Liz today."

"Oh? And how is she?" Some element in his tone and expression, though both were models of politeness, brought color to Fran's cheeks. As usual, she was perfectly transparent to him. He knew she was ill at ease and just making conversation.

"She seems to be happy. I suspect she is enjoying herself bossing her sister around."

Fran still found it hard to believe her aunt had made so little fuss when she learned her niece was moving into a house leased by Jonathan Talbot. The lack of opposition was puzzling, yet Fran didn't doubt her aunt's affection: it was there in the infrequent letters and the occasional long distance telephone call. Either Jonathan had made an indelibly positive effect that one time he had talked to her, or she trusted Fran implicitly.

Larry returned just as Fran was about to exhaust the subject of her aunt's letter. Fran left the two men soon after, with the excuse that she had some reading to do.

Some time later after she had turned off her reading light and settled down in bed to go to sleep, she heard the unmistakable sound of the diesel engine in Jonathan's Mercedes. Where was he going at this hour of the night? No doubt he felt the need of female companionship and was going to seek it with either Eleanor or Anne. A little demon with sharp teeth gnawed away at Fran's insides until finally she fell asleep.

# Chapter Seven

In the soft lighting of her room, the pale bronze satin gleamed richly, highlighting every curve of her slender body. Fran had taken time tonight to use the curling wand on her gold-streaked tawny hair, and it was a mass of waves and loose curls tumbling about her shoulders.

Turquoise eyes wide with shy daring and excitement and the sapphire and diamond ring were the only touches of brilliant color in a picture of brown tones. A single gold chain emphasized the smooth brown column of her neck, and her tanned arms and shoulders were bare except for the tiny satin rope straps.

Staring somewhat aghast at her reflection in the mirror, Fran realized for the first time just how much she was demanding of herself. Now there would be no chance of blending into the background at the party. She would be highly visible in her ultrasophisticated dress, and would have to muster the poise and outward confidence to go along with it. The thought brought a proud tilt to her head.

*Come now!* she lectured herself severely, you've stood up on a stage in front of hundreds of people and you never felt this nervous. That may be true, an inner voice answered, but tonight is different.

And it *was* different in a way she didn't analyze other than to candidly admit that she didn't want to let Jonathan down in front of his social equals and friends. He'd been unstinting in his generosity toward her, opening vistas she hadn't even imagined before, and now she wanted him to be proud of her. And what was more, she wanted him to notice her as a woman and find her no less attractive or desirable than her rivals.

*Rivals!* What was she thinking! How absurd to put herself in the same category with Eleanor and Anne, even in her private thoughts.

Taking up a flimsy shawl of woven gold metallic threads and a tiny gold evening purse, both accessories selected by Eleanor, she was ready to go downstairs and meet the inspection of Jonathan and Larry. Suddenly she was scared to undergo the scrutiny of those gray eyes that always seemed to look right through her ineffectual attempts at self-defense. What if he didn't like the dress? What if he thought she looked ridiculous in it?

Fighting to control fears that eroded her tenuous self-confidence, Fran carefully descended the handsome staircase in her very high-heeled sandals, grateful that truth was contrary to fiction in this instance and there was no handsome male down below watching her, because surely she would have stumbled, fallen and broken her neck.

By the time she had reached the bottom, the erratic beating of her heart had slightly calmed, and no one seeing her would suspect the insecurity gripping her insides as she walked across the hall and into the formal living room, from which she heard masculine voices.

It would have been immensely satisfying to say something witty and sophisticated, but she was lucky to utter "Am I late?" though she knew she wasn't. Both men stood at her entry, but she looked at Larry first, reading admiration in his open, honest face—ignoring for a moment the muttered ejaculation from Jonathan which she would not be able to interpret until she saw his face.

Uncertain of what to expect, she turned her wide questioning eyes to him only to note a total lack of any reaction other than the conventional approval a woman finds on the face of her escort when she enters a room ready for a party. For a few seconds she was so disappointed she felt like crying out her frustration. Only pride saved her.

"Do you like my dress?" she asked, feigning coyness and turning around slowly so that the light gleamed on each satin curve.

A small nerve twitched near one hard jaw in a face that had all the animation of a carved mahogany mask. "I think Eleanor may have something to answer for, turning you loose in a dress like that," he mused, his gray eyes sliding over every inch of her.

"What Jonathan is too bull-headed to admit is that he's afraid he's going to have to fight off every male at the party tonight, including me. And he's right!" Larry's gallantry lifted Fran's spirits and eased the strange tension introduced by her entrance.

The pale green Mercedes sedan was parked in readiness in the driveway. Larry swung open the rear door and gestured invitingly. "Here, Fran, sit in the back with me."

Iron fingers gripped her arm before she could comply. "Sorry, old pal, you're out of luck," Jonathan said brusquely, leaving Fran little choice other than to slide into the front seat, a little dazed by the electrical undercurrents.

"You know the gorgeous Anne ain't gonna be pleased with yours truly," Larry grumbled from the back seat, the first indication to Fran that Anne Taylor would be attending the party with them.

At the Casa Marina Jonathan pulled up in front of the awninged entrance and turned off the engine. Looking over his shoulder at Larry, he apparently engaged in a silent war of wills which he won. Larry groaned his capitulation.

"Okay, you win, old sport, but I'm warning you she's going to be unhappy with the substitution and damage my tender ego." His lack of enthusiasm was obvious as he opened the door and went inside the hotel lobby.

The silence was almost tangible as Jonathan turned sideways behind the wheel and slid an arm along the back of the seat. Fran breathed in sharply and looked up at him when his hand dropped and toyed with the satin rope, which threatened to droop down her arm unless she sat very erect.

The guarded expression had lifted, and he was looking down at the shadowy cleavage between her breasts. Unhurriedly, his gaze roamed over the firm thrust of her breasts against the satin, and then over the bareness of her smooth golden brown neck and shoulders. His husky voice brought myriad pinpricks of sensation.

"Do you have any idea what you do to a man in that dress? I'd bet my life you don't." His free hand rose from the wheel where it was resting and went down to trace the low neckline where it plunged to a deep vee between her breasts. The light touch of those lean fingers against her skin was tantalizing, and Fran looked down in horrified amazement at the visible reaction of her body. Her nipples tingled and hardened until they stood out clearly against the lustrous fabric.

Deep satisfaction in his soft laugh brought hot color to her face. Very gently and deliberately he rubbed a fingertip against each sensitive nipple, sending shock waves through her, and then brought the hand up to curve along her flushed cheek, forcing her to look up into his gray eyes molten with an intense emotion.

"Keep in mind, my little siren, I'm only human."

His lips lowered to hers, and they weren't so undemanding this time. Her initial shock faded immediately and she made no effort to stop him. On the contrary, both hands lifted hesitatingly to the taut muscles of his shoulders and stroked along them to the back of his neck where they delved timidly into the crisp dark hair.

Her lips softened under the hunger of his and then parted to admit the invasion of his tongue, which sought and found hers in an intimacy of exploded sensations that swept aside all consciousness of time and place. No one existed except Jonathan and herself, and the swelling tide of emotion bore her along so swiftly she clung tightly to Jonathan to keep from being submerged and drowning.

Suddenly, he stopped kissing her and pulled her so tightly against his chest she could hardly breathe. His heartbeat was a mighty drumbeat in his chest and his breathing rapid, as if he'd just swum laps in the pool. Then he released her with an abruptness that brought a sharp pang of rejection, especially when she saw the reason.

Larry and Anne were coming through the big entrance doors of the hotel, and Jonathan obviously didn't want them to see Fran in his arms. The slight produced by that realization was followed in fast succession by an insight so surprising that it took every ounce of self-discipline to keep up a polite front as Larry and Anne settled themselves into the back seat.

She had *wanted* Jonathan to kiss her! And what was more, she hadn't felt the least revulsion either during or after the kiss, nor did she feel any guilt for the passion of her response. The discovery was so all-encompassing she wished she had time to be alone and examine it with all its implications.

All too soon they arrived at Eleanor's house, one of the most beautiful and admired of the old Conch houses on the small island and touted by the guides of the Conch Train tour as an example of "bahamian architecture in its purest form." Located on a large corner lot, the house had been constructed in the late 1800s by an enterprising man who helped to introduce the sponge industry to Key West.

Three months ago, anyone informing Fran she would be attending one of the much-publicized galas in this house as a guest would promptly have been categorized lunatic. Now that the moment had arrived when she would have to face Jonathan's social equals in their own familiar habitat, she was stricken with nervousness and clutched his arm as if he might abandon her.

The party was centralized in the spacious backyard, a tropical wonderland with cleverly arranged lights creating an atmosphere of intimacy in spite of the large number of people. A full bar attended by a white-jacketed bartender was set up off to one side. Tables laden with food were kept replenished by several uniformed young men.

Later in the evening there would be live music for dancing on the large flagstone patio, but in the meantime taped music from concealed speakers flooded the whole beautifully landscaped area and mingled with the sounds of conversation and laughter.

For the first hour, Fran moved beside Jonathan from one small group to another while he introduced her as his fiancée. A few of the people she was able to connect with well-known houses, but for the most part they all

blended rather anonymously as polite, fashionable
strangers. Surprise was evident, especially in the faces
of the women, but the eyes of the men showed envy as
well as approval of Jonathan's surprise fiancée.

Eleanor's voice preceded her as she swept toward
them in a stunning black and white hostess gown.
"Have you two had something to eat yet?" Urging
them to sample the food, she surged off to mingle with
other guests, obviously in her element entertaining her
friends.

"You're doing fine," Jonathan assured in a low voice
just for Fran's ears as he led her in the direction of one
of the tables Eleanor had pointed out. Surprisingly, the
food looked really appetizing to Fran, who'd felt sure
she wouldn't be able to eat anything at all at the party.
She helped herself to lobster salad, huge fresh mush-
rooms stuffed with oyster dressing, and a delicious
concoction of marinated shrimp, water chestnuts and
artichoke hearts.

"Hm, this all looks good," she said with genuine
enthusiasm and received an amused glance from Jonathan.

"Nothing diminishes your appetite for very long," he
teased, somehow making it complimentary, and suddenly she no longer felt in the least nervous being here
with him among all these socially prominent people,
some of whom were artists, writers and designers of
national or international reputation.

Soon after that, Larry and an obviously discontented
Anne Taylor joined them. Fran's first glance at the
other woman's cranberry red gown earlier in the evening had made her glad of the impulse which guided her
in the selection of her own dress, which didn't seem
nearly so daring now that she was here among dozens
of beautifully attired women, glittering with jewels that
dazzled the eye even in such soft lighting.

Somehow, with some extremely adroit maneuvering

on Anne's part, Fran became separated from Jonathan. Aware that she was staying very close to Larry, she finally apologized. "Larry, if I cramp your style, please say so. I've probably met every person here tonight, but right now I couldn't tell you a single name!"

He smiled indulgently at her. "That'll be the day when I complain about you sticking too close to me." He looked as if he might say more, but just at that moment they were distracted by the sound of musical instruments tuning up. The band Eleanor had hired for the evening was about to begin playing. The patio had been cleared for dancing, the tables and chairs removed to a safe distance.

After one careful look, Fran reassured herself that she didn't know any of the musicians, who turned out to be older than the ones who might have recognized her as a member of her old crowd. They were quite good, and she found herself responding immediately to their lively opening number.

One partner after another claimed her to dance, and each time she was disappointed it wasn't Jonathan. When she spied him dancing with Eleanor, and then later with Anne, she determined to give every impression of enjoying herself thoroughly without him. Once, when she was dancing to a song with a disco beat, her partner was a young man named Jim Sloan who was closer to her own age than most of the other men. He was an excellent dancer and clearly reveled in showing off his expertise. Even though Fran had never become involved in the disco dancing craze when it was at its height, she had a good sense of rhythm and was able to attune her movements to his.

Gradually the other dancers stopped, moved over to the side and gave Fran and Jim the whole patio. The attention spurred Jim to new heights of innovation and by the time the dance was over and everyone was applauding appreciation, Fran was gasping for breath.

The music changed to a slow number, and Jim kept his arm around her waist.

"I'll have this dance with my fiancée, Jim, if you don't mind." Jonathan's cold voice intimated that he would have the dance whether Jim minded or not.

Fran had been hoping all evening Jonathan would claim her for a dance, and now that it had finally happened, he looked anything but pleased about the prospect. She held herself stiffly as his arm went around her waist but soon gave up the struggle not to respond as he pulled her close against him. He was a superb dancer and she moved effortlessly in step with him, conscious of the hard, muscled length of him against her.

"Why are you mad at me?" she ventured finally, sneaking a look up at him.

He pulled her a little closer so that she could feel her thighs pressed against his. "I didn't bring you here to share you with every man at the party."

The injustice of the remark rankled, and she tried without success to pull away from him. "Of all the nerve. If I waited for *you* to dance with me, I'd be a wallflower."

He didn't answer and that irritated her even more. As if she didn't have eyes in her head and hadn't seen him dancing with Anne and Eleanor. When the music ended, she said quickly, "If you'll excuse me, I have to find the ladies room," and left him without a backward glance.

It wasn't altogether an excuse to get away from him. The elegantly appointed powder room on the ground floor had several women waiting their turn, and by the time she returned to the outside, neither Jonathan nor Larry was in sight. Feeling at a loss, she strolled toward a gigantic banyan tree situated to the left near a high brick wall which enclosed the entire backyard. The massive trunk of the tree was at least six feet in diameter, a size not at all uncommon in Key West. She planned to sit on a small wrought iron bench near it.

Her footsteps made no noise on the damp grass, and she had almost reached the bench when she realized there were people behind the tree. About to retrace her footsteps before she could be discovered and suspected of eavesdropping, she froze at the sound of Eleanor's voice.

"She won't give you up without a fight. Not after the way you've led her on."

"Come on, Eleanor, this is the twentieth century! She's a silly little fool if she expects me to *marry* her. Any man will take what is freely offered."

Jonathan's voice! And the low laugh Fran knew so well, but now harsh with contempt. Not waiting to hear more, she sped back toward the patio, ears echoing with what she'd just heard. They were talking about *her!* How humiliating to be discussed that way!

"Fran, is anything wrong?"

Out of nowhere came her salvation in the guise of Larry's concerned face.

"I don't feel very well," she said truthfully. Her insides were heaving with reaction to Jonathan's words, and she needed desperately to get away from the party before she had to face him again.

"Could you take me home, Larry?"

He looked undecided. "Sure, but can you wait just a minute while I find Jonathan and tell him?"

"Please, Larry," she begged desperately. "I think I'm going to be sick."

He looked closely at her white face and relented without further argument, ushering her through the house and out to the car, which was parked some distance down the street. Fortunately, he had a duplicate key of his own, since he too used the car.

Only after they had pulled away from the curb was Fran able to relax, certain now of being able to get home and safely inside her room without having to make any explanations to Jonathan, who always had that uncanny ability to read her mind. When they reached Garrett House, Larry made a move to get out of the car, but Fran stopped him.

"Please. Go on back to the party and explain to Eleanor and—Jonathan that I got ill all at once and talked you into bringing me home. I'm going straight to bed. I'll probably be fine in the morning."

"Are you sure you'll be all right?" He was plainly reluctant to leave her.

"I'm sure. And if we just disappear together, they won't know what to think. I'll wake Marie or Joanna if I need help."

Her logic was unassailable, and she was finally able to convince him. Locking the front door behind her, she listened for the sound of the car pulling out of the driveway and then succumbed totally to the terrible, all-consuming hurt. How could Jonathan talk about her in that hard, contemptuous way as if she meant nothing in the world to him. She just couldn't stand the pain his words had inflicted on her heart. It was unbearable.

Somehow she managed to get upstairs and out of her clothes, a great numbing inertia spreading through her, blotting out the pain. The dress fell to the floor in a shimmering heap; delicate wisps of undergarments and stockings followed. Naked, she climbed into the bed, wanting nothing but to hunch up under the covers and forget the confusion in her mind.

Suddenly, she remembered the ring and tore it off her finger. She raised her arm in a violent gesture as if to throw the lovely piece of jewelry with all her might against the opposite wall. Instead, she slowed her movement at the last minute so that it fell near the door, unharmed.

With that, something crumpled inside her, and great gasping sobs convulsed her body until she was too exhausted to cry any longer. Her face streaked with tears, she finally fell asleep, whimpering now and then like a brokenhearted child.

Some time later her door opened quietly, admitting a streak of light from the landing. Someone bent with a low exclamation and picked up the ring from the floor. The tall man looked around the room, noting the heap of discarded clothing on the floor, the high-heeled sandals which had been kicked off and left wherever they landed.

He walked over to the bed, leaned down and studied the girl's face, troubled even in her sleep. With a sigh, he bent lower and kissed her gently on the furrowed brow, stood and laid the ring on the bedside table before leaving the room as soundlessly as he had entered.

The next morning Fran awoke with the dull sense that something was wrong. She was lying on her side facing the bedside table and saw the ring there, the small diamonds fiery with light. Puzzled, she wondered how it had gotten there and then with a rush of recollection all of last night swamped her. The excitement of dressing up, the glamorous party like something out of a movie rather than real, the conversation she'd overheard between Eleanor and Jonathan—

*She's a silly little fool if she expects me to marry her! Any man will take what is freely offered.* Those harsh words were branded into her brain, guaranteed to haunt her for the rest of her life. Last night she'd intended to sort the whole jumble out, but had given in to her grief instead, and eventually had fallen asleep in exhaustion.

What greatly puzzled her was what she had done or said to give Eleanor the impression she expected Jonathan to marry her just because they were pretending to be engaged. Had Jonathan told Eleanor the truth about the engagement after he had refused her the right to tell Larry? And what had Fran "offered" Jonathan that he couldn't be blamed for taking? Had he interpreted her response to his kiss as an open invitation?

As much as she pondered these questions, there were no answers forthcoming, but there was a steeling of her resolve to get things absolutely clear between herself and Jonathan. She hadn't asked for this rather bizarre situation where she lived upon his hospitality, and she no longer intended to feel obligated toward him, not if he was going to talk about her like that. At any time he agreed to let her go out and live on her own, she was more than willing. In the meantime, she must make it plain to him that she did not expect him to marry her, nor was she "offering" him her body, should he be under that mistaken impression.

Her attention was drawn back to the ring. How had it gotten there on the table? She remembered throwing it on the carpet last night. Larry must have checked on her at some time during the night and found it. He had been so worried about her last night, so reluctant to leave her alone at the house.

Reluctantly she slid the ring back on her finger and was about to get out of bed when a light tap sounded on her door. Some presentiment told her who it was, the last person in the world she wanted to face at this particular moment, especially in her present state of being naked in bed.

"Who is it?" she called out, but Jonathan apparently thought she had said "Come in." He gave her a searching look as he walked inside the room, pushing the door closed behind him.

"How do you feel? Larry said you suddenly got ill last night at the party."

His concern seemed genuine, but Fran could no longer afford the luxury of trusting him. He looked

119

unbelievably virile in tight denim jeans and a navy tee shirt, and she wondered irrelevantly why he was dressed like that.

"It must have been something I ate. But I feel fine today. In fact, I was just about to get up and put on a swimsuit."

His eyes moved over her figure, suggestively outlined under the thin sheet. She blushed, wondering if he knew she was naked and then realized that he must, since her shoulders were completely bare. She held her breath as he came over and sat down on the edge of the bed, so close she could feel his hip pressing against her leg.

"Fran, why didn't you come and tell me you were sick." His eyes probed her face. She felt terribly vulnerable under that scrutiny.

"You weren't anywhere around, and besides I didn't want to take you away from the party." She forced her eyes to meet his, realizing that her opportunity to clarify things between them had come more quickly than she could possibly have expected. If only she could manage to sound offhand.

"The party was fun. It's just too bad we have to pretend this engagement thing. . . ."

"Why?" The question came like a bark, and he looked about as friendly as a predator about to attack.

"Jim Sloan was a lot of fun. . . . He's a terrific dancer, isn't he?"

Jonathan stood up abruptly and moved a few steps away from the bed, glaring at her. "Jim Sloan's a notorious playboy, and I wouldn't permit you to have anything to do with him even if we weren't—engaged."

Obviously she had accidentally hit a sore spot with Jonathan by mentioning Jim Sloan. They must be old enemies or something. At least she had made a beginning in letting him know she didn't expect him to burden himself permanently with her.

"Where are you going dressed like that?"

He still looked extremely annoyed, and for a moment she thought he might just stride out of her room without even answering. "I had thought we might sail out to the reef and do some snorkeling, if you felt up to it."

"I'd love to!"

In her excitement Fran sat up, forgetting too late that she had on nothing under the sheet. Grabbing it up to cover her bare breasts, she watched Jonathan as he walked quickly to the door and grasped the doorknob in one hand. He seemed to want to avoid looking at her, and she perversely was determined to make him do so.

"It won't take me five minutes to get ready," she assured, and then, as he was about to exit through the door, "Jonathan?"

Giving the impression of reluctance, he stopped and looked back over his shoulders, his eyes moving over the tawny mop of curls and the bare shoulders, the hands clutching the sheet up to her breasts.

"Who else is going?" Fran asked breathlessly.

His shoulders moved slightly under the close-fitting tee shirt, calling her attention to their muscular breadth. "I had in mind a party of two, but I'm sure Larry and Anne can be talked into going along." The door closed abruptly behind him.

# Chapter Eight

Sailing was just as exhilarating as Fran always imagined it would be. Even Anne's rather obvious attempts to make her feel like an outsider couldn't lessen her enjoyment, and she was thrilled beyond words when Jonathan offered to let her handle the wheel.

"Do you think I can do it right?" she asked hesitantly, and then, overcome by the eagerness to give it a try, slipped into his place behind the big stainless steel helm—a lithe brown figure in a purple nylon suit which molded to the lovely curves of her fit body like a second skin. While totally unconscious of the beautiful picture she made, she *was* conscious of the deeply tanned sinew and muscle of the man close beside her in a brief dark suit that hugged his lean hips.

Side by side, Fran and Jonathan looked like a sun god and goddess in contrast to the other couple, who were making every effort to shield themselves from the brilliant sunshine beaming into the cockpit of the sleek fiberglass sloop. Anne wore a floppy-brimmed hat, white slacks and a long-sleeved white gauze blouse unbuttoned to reveal the abbreviated top of her black bikini. She eyed Fran's brown skin with marked disapproval and made frequent applications of sunscreen lotion to her own fair skin.

Larry wore green bathing trunks of the old-fashioned boxer shorts variety and a plaid shirt. Fran was relieved when he yielded to Jonathan's advice and went down below to find a hat to protect his flushed face from the sun's hot rays. His skin was the sensitive kind which burned rather than tanned.

Hardly able to contain her elation at the steady surging motion of the boat as it cut smoothly through the crystal clear water, Fran smiled at Jonathan, her eyes narrowed between long gold-tipped lashes to screen out the glare of the sun. "I love sailing!"

"I thought you would," he said softly for her ears only, and something leaped from his eyes to hers, born of the mutual joy they both felt at this moment.

A fluttering sound from aloft called her attention back to steering, which wasn't nearly so difficult as she had at first feared. They were pointed generally in the direction of the reef, and all she had to do was keep the wind in the sails so that they didn't flap or rustle, as they had begun to do just now when she'd forgotten everything in her absorption with the expression in Jonathan's eyes. For a crazy moment she had felt like they were the only two people in the world, a fancy she could only explain as a product of her excitement.

The conversation among the four of them earlier during the time it had taken to motor the forty-foot sloop from the private yacht basin off Roosevelt Avenue out into the deep water had brought some surprising revelations to Fran, as she realized just how little she knew about Jonathan. Larry and Anne had questioned him about the SORC races that year. They both expressed surprise that he hadn't participated in them as he usually did.

"I was just too busy," he explained with a shrug, choosing not to elaborate further.

"What does SORC mean?" Fran asked in the silence that followed, and was immediately made to feel insufferably ignorant by the look Anne gave her.

"Southern Ocean Racing Conference," Larry explained quickly, intercepting the look. "You mean you didn't know old Jonathan here is one of the super yachtsmen in this country?" he teased good-naturedly. "I don't risk my hide with just anybody, you know."

Anne had seemed to take particular delight in Fran's ignorance of Jonathan's yacht racing background. "Where Jonathan and I grew up in Maine, we learned to sail before we learned to ride a tricycle."

That remark was interesting for several reasons. It suggested that Jonathan and Anne had known each other since childhood, even though Fran's impression of Anne definitely didn't place her in the "girl next door" category. What was also puzzling was Anne's behavior since coming aboard the boat. She had settled herself comfortably in the cockpit and offered no assistance in untying mooring lines and standing by to see that the gleaming white hull wasn't grazed by a piling as it backed from the slip.

In contrast, Fran had been all eagerness, helping to remove the sail covers, and once out into the open water following Jonathan's explicit directions when the time came to hoist the white dacron sails, which crackled like paper. Why, she wondered now as she had earlier, didn't Anne show any interest in the handling of the boat if she had indeed grown up sailing? Curiosity getting the best of her, she tried to phrase a question both tactful and to the point.

"Anne, do you sail a lot?" Something in the quality

of the silence made Fran suspect she was the only one among the four of them who didn't already know the answer.

"No, actually I don't. The wind and sun dry out my skin." The full red lips tightened a little as Anne looked from Jonathan to Larry, both of whom were resolutely silent. "Besides, I have a tendency to get seasick unless I take Dramamine tablets ahead of time."

"Oh, that's too bad!" The sympathy in Fran's voice was genuine, and she wasn't deserving of the scorching glare she received from Anne's blue eyes shielded behind enormous sunglasses.

"The only reason I came along today was that Jonathan was so *insistent.*" Her meaning was clear even if she didn't spell it out in so many words: Jonathan didn't want to be stuck alone with Fran.

What had he said earlier to Fran? *I'm sure Anne and Larry can be talked into going along.* The bubble of her elation burst into a thousand fragments as she remembered with sickening clarity the conversation she had overheard between Jonathan and Eleanor the previous evening. How could she have pushed it so completely out of her mind today? Last night the hurt and rejection had been so overpowering she had fled from the party like a wounded animal desperate to find a safe place to stanch the flow of life's blood.

Gone now was the feeling of harmony, the exulting sensation of motion and space and people all yielding to a common unity of purpose. Fran felt herself a separate, isolated human being. The sun was still hot and bright, the ocean dazzled her eyes with millions of brilliant diamond pinpricks, the breeze blew her hair back from her face and brushed sensuously against her heated skin, but her former exhilaration was gone. Its edge had been dulled by the reminder of just how equivocal was her position among these people in the cockpit. They belonged together. She was the outsider.

"Here, Jonathan, you take the wheel," she said tersely and before he could reply moved over to perch beside Larry, who had uncomplainingly taken the least comfortable side of the cockpit on each tack, always giving Anne the leeward side.

Instinctively she knew Jonathan was aware of the deflation of her spirits, so high just moments ago. She risked a glance at him under the pretext of looking all around them for other boats. His jaw was rigid, his mouth set into a hard line contrary to the relaxed posture of his body as he leaned back, resting his elbows on the deck behind him and steering the boat with his bare feet. A surge of awareness coursed through her at the sight of the indolent maleness of him sprawled there, latent power in the lean brown hardness of his long body.

"How much farther?"

Anne's petulant question came as a relief, breaking the spell that seemed to lock Fran's gaze on Jonathan. She looked away from him, willing her disturbed pulse to return to normal.

"Not far at all," came the laconic response from the man behind the steering wheel.

"I can see the reef!" Fran exclaimed suddenly, leaning over the side, everything else temporarily forgotten in the excitement of seeing the dark green and brown of the coral formations beneath them now. The turquoise water was so crystal clear she could see straight to the bottom as she peered over the side of the boat.

"Careful, kid," Larry warned good-naturedly, grasping her by the waist with both hands. "If you're not careful, you'll be over head first."

"Larry, you take the wheel," Jonathan ordered curtly.

Larry removed his hands from Fran's waist and obeyed, not commenting on the steel in his friend's voice. Fran straightened, watching Jonathan move swiftly up the side of the boat to the foredeck.

"Okay, Fran," he barked, "take the jib sheet off the cleat and get ready to release it when I tell you to."

Thanks to his instructions earlier, she knew the jib sheet was the long nylon line connected to a bottom corner of the triangular foresail, and she quickly followed the instructions, faintly apprehensive that she might do something wrong.

"Okay, Larry, head her into the wind."

The boat responded immediately to the twist of the wheel, and the sails made a deafening flapping noise aloft. Fran wondered if Larry had misunderstood the instructions and done the wrong thing.

"Let it go, Fran."

She quickly unwound the line from the spool-shaped stainless steel winch and watched breathlessly as Jonathan gave several vigorous tugs and brought the flapping jib to the deck where he took several short lengths of elastic cord and secured it to the lifeline.

Next he stepped with practiced sureness up on the low cabin top and deftly released the mainsail halyard. The big sail slid down the mast, and the boat was soon just drifting through the water, having lost most of its momentum now that resistance to the wind was gone.

During the next few minutes, Jonathan gave instructions in a crisp voice, and in short order the mainsail was tied in several places to the boom, all the lines neatly coiled, and the anchor let out. Fran released a sigh of relief.

"That was pretty exciting!" she marveled. "Everything happens at once."

"You get used to it," Jonathan replied. "Two people who know what they're doing can run this boat with no problem." He must have read her mind because he added, "I could have you trained in no time at all."

Her heart lurched crazily at the expression in his eyes

which belied the matter-of-factness of his voice. Why did he say things like that to her, tempting her to hope there might be a future to their relationship, when she *knew* his real feelings about her. Hadn't she heard the scorn in his voice when he referred to her as a "silly little fool"?

There was no time now to brood over these disturbing questions. Jonathan removed the swimming ladder from a locker beneath the starboard cockpit seat and fixed it firmly in place over the side. Next he took out ski belts, masks, flippers and snorkels.

"I know we can all swim," he said pleasantly, but in a tone that brooked no disagreement, "but the safety regulations say everybody should wear a flotation vest or belt. Larry, Anne, you two can go first."

Several minutes later, he turned his attention to Fran. "Do you know how to breathe through a snorkel?"

She nodded, anticipation overcoming every other emotion and adding a sparkle to her eyes which made them even more akin to the turquoise sea on which the yacht floated with a gentle bobbing motion. She had used a snorkel several times in the past few years, joining expeditions out to the reef with groups of friends who had pooled their resources to rent a motor boat.

"Here, let me help you do that," Jonathan said when she took the ski belt from him and began to buckle it around her waist. The nearness of him made her suck in her breath as he bent a little in front of her. She could smell the warm muskiness of his flesh and restrained a strong urge to trail her hand along the muscular brownness of the broad shoulders at eye level. It was a decided relief when he straightened and transferred his attention to fastening his own belt.

Once in the water she was lost to everything except

the fascinations of the sea world around her. The variety of shapes and textures of the coral formations was a source of infinite wonder. Huge dense boulder-like structures, called brain corals because of the meandering pathways on the surface resembling those of the human brain, contrasted strikingly with the slender structured velvet-green elkhorn coral, whose branches, some extending to a height of at least ten feet, were reminiscent of the mighty horns after which it was named.

One variety of coral reminded Fran of a cactus, having many stubby little projections, while another was similar to lichen growing on the bark of a tree, layered and ruffled, only much larger. The most fascinating coral, though, were the ones shaped like gigantic fans, undulating snakelike with the water currents at the bottom of the ocean.

The rainbow colors satisfied her gypsy love of vivid hues: dark green grew next to pale green; aqua and pale pink nestled unconcernedly beside flaming orange. Exotically-patterned fish darted into sight and then glided into the dense maze of the reef. Now and then a movement on the ocean floor drew her attention to the iridescent glitter of a spiny lobster.

She had no idea how long she had been gliding across the surface of the water, gazing downward, when a touch on her shoulder startled her back to reality. She lifted her head to find Jonathan close beside her. Smiling, he pointed. Following the direction of his hand, she was amazed to see how far she had come. From this distance, the boat looked small.

Raising her head above water, she pulled the snorkel out of her mouth and held it in one hand, pushing the mask up on her forehead with the other as she tread water beside him, the ski belt making her buoyant. Her enthusiasm was too great to contain.

"Isn't it just *incredible* down there? I think I could stay out here forever, just floating around and watching!"

His eyes moved over her enthralled face, and his stern features softened into a pleased smile. "For a while I thought your destination might be Miami. By the time we get back to the boat, it'll be time for lunch."

Settling her mask back into place and putting the snorkel in her mouth, Fran thought fleetingly how natural and right it seemed to her at this moment to have Jonathan in the water beside her. His nearness wasn't in the least an intrusion. If anything, it intensified her pleasure to know he must not have been far away from her the whole time, noticing perhaps the same shapes and colors and movements as she.

Anne and Larry were already aboard the boat when Fran and Jonathan arrived there. Fran was still under the sea's enchanting spell, and couldn't contain the expression of her wonder. In spite of what the others might think, she didn't care if enthusiasm made her unsophisticated.

Jonathan put up an awning to shade the cockpit and brought the picnic hamper up from the cabin where it had been stowed. While Fran unpacked its contents, he went back down the companionway steps and handed up cans of soft drink and beer from the icebox.

Fran was ravenous. Joanna and Maria had packed sandwiches made with thin slices of roast beef and swiss cheese. There were also pickles, Greek peppers, boiled eggs and raw vegetables to dip into a horseradish and sour cream dressing. Everything tasted so much better than usual that Fran felt the need to utter her appreciation to the world in general.

"I was wondering if you always have an appetite like that," Anne remarked disparagingly. She herself had eaten little and had requested a diet drink.

"She does."

Jonathan and Larry spoke in unison, bringing a blush to Fran's cheeks. But their expressions as they regarded her slim figure held such approval she felt no uncomfortable embarrassment. It was true that she enjoyed food, but then burned up a lot of energy in exercise.

After the remains of the lunch had been cleared away, the paper plates and empty aluminum cans placed in a plastic garbage bag, Fran lay back drowsily, reflecting to herself that she wished this day would never have to end. She was having such fun.

Then someone mentioned Eleanor's party and reality flooded back, bringing with it the despairing memory of the conversation between Eleanor and Jonathan. Suddenly she realized Anne was speaking directly to her.

"Jim Sloan was quite taken with you, Fran. He was beside himself when you disappeared all of a sudden. He wondered if he had said or done something to upset you."

Fran sat up, smothering a powerful urge to wipe the smug smile right off Anne's face with the truth: that her exit had nothing to do with Jim Sloan, who had no importance to Fran one way or another. Instead, she conjured a smile and managed to make her voice flippant.

"I hope I get a chance to see him soon so I can put his mind at ease."

Anne looked excessively pleased with that answer, Larry appeared uncomfortable, and Jonathan retreated into a forbidding silence that lasted during the entire sail back. They were motoring into the harbor when he spoke again, addressing his words to Larry.

From their exchange she learned that Jonathan was leaving early in the morning on business and would be gone a week or two—he wasn't really sure at the present time. When he returned, he would bring some friends back with him, Ellen and Bill Alden.

Anne chimed in at this news, making it evident she, too, knew the couple. Once again Fran was the only outsider, and she miserably wished herself a thousand miles away, or at least back in her old life with people on her own social level who accepted her for who and what she was. At the moment they were motoring past the pier at Mallory Square, and without any warning she was besieged with a powerful longing for all that she had given up at Jonathan's insistence. How sure of herself she had been during those carefree days when the inevitable end of each day was a stroll along that pier at Sunset. Now she didn't belong anywhere and never knew what rested beyond the next moment— what unknown emotions and dangers would confront her.

If only she could go back—

Jonathan was already gone when Fran arose early the next morning and jogged to Memorial Beach. Relief at knowing she wouldn't have to meet the disrupting impact of his gray eyes for a week or two was mixed with disappointment that Jonathan had left without even saying good-bye to her. Maybe now, she reflected wistfully, things would return to an even routine with just she, Larry and the two housekeepers present in the house.

During the weekdays and on Saturday she continued to work for Eleanor in the shop. With no classes to attend until summer session began in a few weeks, she had extra time on her hands and spent much of it with Larry. Although it soon became evident he had little need of her services, she found the restoration work on the houses fascinating; and Larry seemed not only willing but delighted to tutor her in the rudiments of architectural design. Whenever possible, she helped him by running errands.

According to her wish, life settled into a comfortable routine and she was able to push into the back of her mind any insecurities about her present life. As had been her habit for years, she pushed her body to the limit in rigorous exercise. By the time she turned off her lamp at night, she was tired and able to fall immediately into a deep, restful sleep undisturbed by dreams of a tall man with arresting gray eyes and a disruptive presence.

In a few days she found the pretense of her engagement to Jonathan less and less credible, the sapphire ring its only tangible reminder. In a moment of confidentiality, she told Larry, as she had wanted to do in the beginning, that the engagement was a sham to discourage gossip among Jonathan's friends. The revelation had the effect of rupturing some former barrier in her relationship with Larry, and his affectionate overtures toward her became more frequent and open.

She remembered with a tinge of uneasiness Jonathan's warning that Larry was in danger of falling in love with her, dismissing it as ridiculous. Larry just liked her the way she liked him: as a close friend. When he put his arms around her, as he had come to do more often lately, and kissed her gently on the mouth, she found his show of affection warm and comforting, nothing more. There was none of the pronounced sensory response Jonathan could produce with the most casual touch—or even by coming close to her.

Then when Jonathan had been gone almost two weeks, she learned to her dismay that his prediction about Larry's emotional disposition in regard to her was unerring. After dinner one evening, she and Larry were sitting on the patio talking while he sipped a brandy with his coffee. Fran had been asking him questions about how he had decided to become an architect, and what his future plans for his career entailed.

Suddenly, the conversation took on distressingly intimate overtones that shocked her. Larry's soft brown eyes were brimming with emotion as he declared his deep feelings for her.

"Larry!" she protested, still unable to believe what she had heard. "You can't love me—*like that.*"

"I'm sorry, Fran, that the idea upsets you, but I *do* love you 'like that,' as you put it. I'd like nothing more in the world to marry you."

She was at a total loss as to what to say next. His emotion touched her deeply, but she didn't love him, or at least she didn't think she did. Not for anything in the world would she consciously say or do anything callous to hurt his feelings, and her sensitive features mirrored the turmoil inside her.

He read her inner struggle and smiled reassuringly. "Don't worry about me, dear. I didn't really expect you to feel the same way I do, not yet, anyway. But I wanted you to know I'm here if you need me. Practically speaking, I'm not poor by a longshot, and you wouldn't want for anything if you married me."

Later that night as she lay in her bed, unable to sleep for going over in her mind the whole conversation, she considered the possibility of accepting Larry's proposal of marriage. After all, she liked him very much and admired his good qualities. He was intelligent and sensitive and certainly not unattractive, even though there was no comparison between him and Jonathan— Abruptly she turned off that train of thought, knowing it was unfair to Larry as well as profoundly disturbing to her peace of mind.

Without reaching any decision, she fell asleep and dreamed not about Larry, but about herself and Jonathan. They were out sailing on the sloop, but this time they were all alone far from the sight of land. For once there were no barriers separating them, just perfect harmony as they worked together to sail the boat. The sensations of freedom and elation were so intense Fran thought her heart might explode from sheer happiness.

Then suddenly, without any explanation, Jonathan was no longer on the boat. Fran didn't know what had happened to him, but she was completely alone in the middle of the huge ocean. There was no end in sight, just total and complete aloneness forever, and she was terribly afraid.

She awoke to find her cheeks wet with tears. The dream was still clear in all its details, the initial sweetness as well as the final terror and desolation. It was totally unlike her to feel the way she did—apathetic and lacking the eagerness to face a new day. After all, it was only a dream.

The sense of despondency remained with her all morning at work. At least she had the afternoon off and wouldn't have to put up a show of cheer. Larry had gone to Miami for the day to consult with an architect noted as an authority on southern house design.

After eating a light lunch of fresh fruit and cottage cheese on the patio, she donned a bikini and took a paperback novel out to the pool area, where she alternately read and dozed for several hours. Waking to find herself hot and thirsty, she left her book open face down on the tiled area surrounding the pool and went into the kitchen to get a glass of something cool to drink. The two sisters were sitting at the kitchen table, making out a list, and Fran overheard a bit of their conversation as she got ice from the refrigerator.

"They should be here about four, Mr. Jonathan said."

"I made up the big front bedroom for his friends."

Was Jonathan coming home today? The prospect jolted her out of the lethargy which had weighed her down all day. An unreasoning panic took control, and she placed the glass of lemonade she had just poured in the sink without even tasting it. She just *couldn't* be here when Jonathan arrived with his friends. After Larry's proposal last night and that disturbing dream, she wasn't ready to face Jonathan. She was afraid of what he might read in her eyes, some truth she hadn't even admitted to herself.

Giving no thought to the book she had left out by the pool beside her lounge chair, she ran up the stairs compelled by a great urgency to escape from the house before it was too late to do so. Blind instinct guided her choices as she reached for worn jeans and a plain cotton knit top. Her hair waved and formed loose curls of its own volition as she gave it a hasty brushing. She didn't bother at all with makeup, and as she left her room and ran down the stairs with the air of someone in a great hurry, she might have been any young woman eagerly on her way for a day of sightseeing in Key West.

Her bicycle, in a storage building at the back of the house, looked like a dear friend as she wheeled it out into the afternoon sun. The tires were a little low on air, but she didn't dare stop now to attend to them. Her immediate aim was to get safely away from the house. Once that was accomplished, she pedaled more slowly, with no destination in mind. The wind felt wonderful on her face and neck, lifting her hair and easing the tension in her body until slowly, gradually, she regained the old sensation of timelessness as she passed along familiar streets of houses set among lush tropical foliage.

Up ahead she saw Smathers Beach, crowded with young people playing volleyball, throwing frisbies, windsurfing, sunbathing, swimming and watching one another. Not long ago she had been one of them, with not a thought of the future, but surprisingly she felt little regret as she bicycled past, noting the usual diverse collection of vans, campers and concession trucks offering tacos and hot dogs parked across the street under tall palm trees.

Passing East Martello Tower, the old brick fort now open to the public as a museum, she rounded a sharp curve and saw the usual assortment of cruising boats anchored in the area of protected water between Key West and Stock Island. At one time she had felt much in common with these hardy people who lived aboard their boats and came ashore in dinghies to buy provisions or to explore the island. She'd imagined that they were free, because they didn't work at regular jobs but sailed from one port to another, managing somehow to support themselves. Now she wondered if she wouldn't grow tired of that kind of life, without a goal or purpose other than arriving at the next place.

Eventually she found herself right in the heart of old Key West, familiar territory over which she had walked and bicycled countless times. By the time she parked her bicycle, she realized for the first time what she intended to do. The genesis of today's action had lain there dormant in her mind ever since the day she'd gone sailing with Jonathan and Larry and Anne. On the way into the harbor, when they passed the Mallory Square pier where people were already beginning to gather, she had experienced a sudden longing to go backward in time.

Today, for the first time in nearly four months, she would go back to Sunset. It was more than just a whim; it was a driving need. Right now she felt so alienated from everything and everybody, cut off from the past and unsure of the future. She had been happy during the period when she was a regular celebrant of the Sunset ritual, capable of picking up a guitar at a moment's notice and bewitching the crowd into gifts of money or, more often, content just to wander along the pier and enjoy the atmosphere.

What she hoped to find or to learn this afternoon was unclear, but she knew now she had been heading in this direction all along, albeit by a circuitous route. Maybe, just *maybe,* she would find herself.

Ambling along Duval Street, she gazed into shop windows without curiosity and then, in order to avoid passing anywhere near Eleanor's shop, ducked off onto a side street before she came to Front Street. On impulse, she stopped and bought a double-dip of pistachio nut ice cream and walked along eating it, getting more than a few interested glances from those she passed. Even in her plain outfit of jeans and a dark knit top, she was a strikingly lovely young woman.

Approaching Mallory Square, she was struck suddenly with understanding of some change in herself she had felt vaguely all afternoon but had not been able to pinpoint. Before, when she saw the old buildings surrounding the square, she had thought little of them except as being rather drab and ugly. Now she knew their history as offices and warehouses in the salvage industry that had been so vital to Key West's early prosperity. Before she had moved into Garrett House, come to know Larry and to develop an interest in Key West architecture, she had paid little attention to the movement to preserve the historical character of the old town section. This afternoon she had noted evidences of this concern and found them to her liking.

She even saw the concrete pier, toward which she was headed, in a different light. Recently she had seen pictures of the old wooden pier which had been replaced because it was rotting to pieces and presented a hazard to safety. The present stout concrete structure was no longer just something she took for granted, but part of the continuum of Key West history.

Fran strolled along the pier in the direction of a young couple who took guitars from frayed black cases and began to play them and sing together. The girl looked no older than seventeen or eighteen, her face free of makeup, her black hair hanging down to her waist. The young man, bearded and not much older than the girl, wore denim clothing incredibly threadbare but clean.

A crowd collected quickly around them as they sang an old Bob Dylan song with a poignant melody, the lyrics of which expressed doubt about the purpose of human existence. The girl's voice rang out sweet and clear: *The answer, my friend, is blowin' in the wind.* Fran herself had sung the refrain many times and always felt pleasurably sad when she did, but now powerful emotions gripped her as she stood in the midst of the shifting, pressing crowd, listening and watching.

Just a short time ago, *she* could have been inside the circle of people, but that was out of the question now. She felt immeasurably separated from the young couple who lived an existence and portrayed a philosophy she had once adhered to. Something had happened to her during the past months to make her realize there was much to learn and experience in her lifetime. Never again would she be able to live idly from day to day with no thought of tomorrow. She had changed. The realization saddened her, prompting a wrenching sense of loss, as if a part of her had been amputated without her knowledge.

The tears that welled and spilled down her cheeks were for the old Fran who was no more, who once was as aimless and carefree as the two young people separated from her by a few feet of space and a barrier of discovery. No matter what happened to her now, if Jonathan turned her out on the street tomorrow, she would never be able to return to this same state of mind.

*Jonathan!*

The name brought a knife-like pain to her chest as she remembered a past Sunset that meant more to her now than any of the others: the afternoon he had forced her to accompany him. She had tried to lose him in the crowd, but that firm hand had remained at her waist, making her breathtakingly aware of him.

In the midst of her grief, Fran felt the force of eyes and looked up, startled. It was too incredible for belief—as if the power of her thoughts had conjured the man dominating them—for directly across from her in the crowd stood the last person she expected to encounter at this particular place and moment. *Jonathan!* Her brain did not concern itself with questions as to how or why he happened to be there, for without warning everything settled into dazzling focus.

*She was in love with Jonathan!*

Overwhelmed with her discovery, which was so painfully obvious to her now, she turned and fled through the crowd, knowing that she couldn't possibly face Jonathan now. He would see the truth in her eyes.

She didn't slow down her pace until she reached the place several blocks away where she had left her bicycle. Her hands trembled so violently that she had difficulty with the combination lock. Every second she felt as if pursuing footsteps would catch up with her, but when she paused and listened, she heard no sound of someone following her.

Jonathan hadn't come after her. The realization deepened the wound in her heart, and she rode through the slowly darkening streets blinded by tears. What a choice irony, she thought bitterly. She had gone to Sunset this afternoon searching for something, an answer to explain the confusion inside her. She'd learned her answer all right, but a lot of good it would do her.

By the time she reached Garrett House, it was nearly dark. She put the bicycle back in the shed and slipped quietly into the house through the back way and up the stairs to her room, her heart pounding with the fear of encountering someone. She didn't want anyone, not even Joanna or Maria, to see her tearstained face.

A gradual calm restored her common sense, and she was able to formulate a rational explanation for Jonathan's presence at Mallory Square. He had obviously arrived home this afternoon with his guests and taken them to Sunset, surely never suspecting that he would see Fran there crying her heart out. It was up to her to conceal from him the true reason.

His face as he had stared at her across the crowd was printed indelibly on her memory. He had looked stern and forbidding and—stricken. She could only hope that her face hadn't been as transparent to him as it so often was—that he didn't know she loved him.

For the present she couldn't afford the luxury of time to examine the secret she had managed so well until now to keep from herself. She had to prepare to face Jonathan and his guests. An instinct of self-preservation led her, for the first time since moving into the house, to turn the big, old-fashioned key in the lock of her door. Later she was glad she had taken the precaution.

After some consideration of the clothes hanging in the armoire, she took out a turquoise silk dress with simple lines and laid it in readiness across the bed. She had showered and just finished drying her hair when she thought she heard a knock at her door. Moving to the open bathroom door, she listened and heard the light tapping again.

"Fran?"

*It was Jonathan!* With wildly pounding heart, she stood silent and watched the door knob turn. One part of her was fervently glad she had locked the door, and the part in disagreement was quickly reduced to surrender. Jonathan must have gone away after discovering that the door was locked.

Fran hadn't taken so much care with her appearance

since the night of Eleanor's big garden party, but the end results tonight were highly successful nevertheless. Her hair waved and curled softly around her face. Turquoise blue eyes were highlighted by a subtle application of eye shadow and mascara. Lips glistened with gloss. The simple elegance of the dress was perfect for the effect she sought: to look older and self-assured.

Her timing was deliberate and fortunate. When she went downstairs, Jonathan was out on the patio with his guests. The presence of strangers helped her get through the first confrontation with him without losing her composure. It also helped that she liked the Aldens at first sight. Ellen Alden was a diminutive woman with flame red hair and a vivacious personality. Bill, exceptionally tall and thin with gaunt, craggy features, made quite a contrast to his wife.

Fran was relieved that there was no embarrassing fuss when Jonathan introduced her as his fiancée. Evidently they had been forewarned and accepted the idea. Nor did she experience awkwardness as she joined in the conversation, most of it about Key West, before dinner was served. Still, she was glad Larry joined them, although looking a bit hurried, it appeared that he had just arrived home from Miami and had rushed in order to be ready in time for dinner.

After he had shaken hands with Bill and hugged Ellen, he sank into a chair next to Fran. She smiled warmly at him, thinking how dear and familiar he was. The welcome evident in her face brought a surge of color to his already ruddy complexion, and instantly she felt a tinge of regret as Larry looked back at her with an expression open for all present to read. Involuntarily Fran glanced over at Jonathan and saw the anger smoldering in his eyes.

Throughout the rest of the evening Larry remained constant in his attentions to her, and she couldn't seem to find it in herself to discourage him, even though it would have been the fair thing to do. As long as he was close by, she felt safe and protected from Jonathan, whose anger glinted in his eyes whenever he looked their way.

Relieved when Ellen and Bill retired to their room, pleading tiredness after a long day, Fran wasted no time in escaping to her own. Once there, though, she was far too pent up to sleep. There was too much to think about, and her thoughts darted like a rat in a cage.

After a while she decided in desperation that reading might help ease her tension and enable her to get to sleep. Remembering the novel she had left down by the pool, she decided to retrieve it since it would no doubt be soaked with dew by morning; and besides, the idea of going outside in the evening coolness appealed strongly. The house was so quiet she could be assured all the rest were asleep.

The short robe she slipped over her nightgown was more for the thought than the actual modesty the thin material provided. Barefoot, she sped noiselessly down the stairs in the dim light from an old-fashioned brass wall fixture.

The bricks of the patio were pleasantly cool and rough under her feet. She padded unhurriedly across the damp grass to the pool, reached the lounge chair she had used earlier in the day and bent over to pick up the paperback book, still open to her place. A sound startled her and she whirled around, her heart lurching with sudden fright.

*"Jonathan!"* she whispered shakily. "You scared the living daylights out of me!"

He stood so close she could have reached out and touched him. He too was barefoot and ready for bed, wearing nothing but a dark robe knotted around the waist and revealing much of his chest.

"I heard you leave your room and thought maybe I'd

get a chance to talk to you without your faithful shadow." The bitter irony in his voice left little doubt that he'd noticed how closely Larry had stuck to her all evening. He wasn't pleased.

Jonathan's proximity was doing wild things to her. Her heartbeat was an erratic thud against her chest wall, and she could feel the blood pulsing in her ears. Her knees felt so strangely weak that she would either have to sit down soon or get away from him.

"I—er, I couldn't sleep and remembered I'd left my book down here this afternoon." She took a half step as if to move past him.

"Don't go," his voice arrested her. "What went on between you and Larry while I was gone?" He seemed to tower over her, and she sensed a puzzled anger in his voice.

It dawned upon her then that Jonathan didn't realize she had told Larry the truth about their phony engagement. Larry's attentive behavior toward her all evening must have appeared disloyal to Jonathan. That was the reason for his anger. She hastened to explain, her voice shaking a little from nervous reaction to his nearness, which was arousing a host of sensations she was coming to expect when he was near.

"Nothing's been 'going on' between Larry and me, as you put it, but you were right about one thing, Jonathan." Her voice was tinged with regret. "Larry *is* getting serious about me. In fact . . . he asked me to marry him."

The tall man in front of her, so close she could have reached out and trailed her fingers across his bare chest, seemed plunged into deep silence, and she realized she still hadn't explained everything.

"In a way, it's my fault, I guess. I told him we weren't really engaged."

The tense silence strained her nerves to breaking point. Why didn't he *say* something? Anything to cover the frantic pounding of her heart! "It would solve your problem of how to explain me, wouldn't it? We wouldn't have to pretend to be engaged any more." Still he said nothing. "Larry would probably make a very good husband, and I wouldn't be on your hands any more. . . ."

The prospect of marrying a man other than Jonathan destroyed what remained of her shaky composure, and the burning in her eyes warned her of the tears that would spill over at any moment. Before Jonathan could agree with her and break her heart wide open, she attempted to brush past him, intending to flee to the sanctuary of her room, where she would succumb totally to her wretchedness.

His hands came out of the pockets of his robe with lightning quickness and grasped her by the shoulders. A whimpering sound in her throat seemed to release something in him, snapping his control, and he closed his arms around her, crushing her against the hard, muscular wall of his chest. With the warmth of his bare flesh against her cheek, her nostrils were invaded by the musky masculine scent of him, and acting on blind instinct she turned her head to press her lips against him.

He groaned deep in his throat and one hand slid up her back to entangle itself in her touseled hair, gently forcing her head back. His heart was pounding as hard as hers now—she could feel the staccato beat against her breasts and the great tension in his hard length as if he were under a strain and exerting prodigious control.

His mouth lowered to hers and moved sensuously, imploringly, asking for a response. She arched closer, hugging him more tightly around the waist, and the urgency of the kiss rapidly increased, his mouth forcing her lips apart to allow the plunging invasion of his tongue.

Her hands gained a new daring and moved up at first

145

shyly and experimentally and then with incalculable delight to stroke the firm muscles of his back. How often watching that powerful brown expanse had she longed to touch him, freely, as she was doing now.

Jonathan's breathing was as shallow and uneven as her own when he pulled his mouth away from the sweet compliance of hers and lowered it to her neck. She shivered with pleasure at this further onslaught, weak and tremulous with the rapturous sensations he was arousing. His breath was hot against her skin as his lips trailed slowly down to the deep vee of her robe, which he parted with a hand that trembled, as though he were as weak as she felt.

She gasped as one hand cupped a breast through the thin material of her nightgown, then felt a curious ache far down in her middle as the hand kneaded the firm roundness gently and thoroughly. When he pressed his mouth to the hard nipple, the piercing delight that shot through her was almost more than she could bear, and she moaned.

Drawing in a long shuddering breath, he straightened and gathered her close against the long length of him, making her aware of his virility and his need for her. Fran writhed against him, wanting him to continue kissing and caressing her, all timidity banished now by the demands of a healthy young body awakened to the sweet, wild music of passion.

"Fran, this situation is becoming intolerable!"

The anguish in the low, muttered words pierced her consciousness and struck deep at the core of the insecurity inside her. Her first thought was that Jonathan had read her emotional discovery that afternoon the way he always seemed to read her mind. Was he afraid to make love to her for fear that she would expect him to marry her?

These thoughts made her go rigid in the crushing vise

of Jonathan's arms, and immediately his hold loosened. With a cry of pain, she pulled away from him and fled across the damp lawn. For the second time in less than twenty-four hours, she was running away from him, and once again he did not follow. That fact seemed to underline her conclusions.

# Chapter Nine

Fran was getting dressed for work when Joanna came up to her room to tell her she was wanted on the telephone.

"Who is it? Is it long distance?" Her first thought was that something must be wrong with Aunt Liz.

"It's a lady, but she didn't say if she was calling long distance." Joanna's reply was typically laconic.

It was Eleanor, and she was calling from New Orleans.

"Fran, I tried to call you yesterday afternoon before I left, but you weren't in, and then last night I was busy. I'd prefer not to go into details on the telephone, but my niece, Deirdre, is going through something of a personal crisis, and her mother is in Europe. I'm probably going to have to be here at least a week. In the meantime, I've just closed up the shop. It's our slow time, anyway. Relax and take a few days off with pay."

Never had an employee been less happy with such news. Because she didn't have an extension in her room, Fran had taken the call in the library. Now she went back upstairs and changed into shorts and a halter top, trying to digest the fact that she would have nowhere to go during the next few days to escape Jonathan.

Leaving her room to go down for breakfast, she met Ellen at the head of the stairs and explained the circumstances of her newly acquired leisure.

"What wonderful news!" Ellen exclaimed, looking genuinely delighted. "Now I won't have to entertain myself today!"

Fran went automatically out to the patio, where she usually had breakfast on weekends, and looked around for some sign of the men. Ellen was following her, talking nonstop, and some of the lighthearted chatter began to sink in.

". . . don't know why one of us didn't think to mention it last night. Nothing would satisfy Bill but to go fishing his first full day here—on one of those big sports fishing boats. Usually I'm game for anything, but not that. Not the *whole* day!"

Ellen's giggle was infectious and Fran relaxed as soon as she realized what the other woman was explaining in her somewhat effusive manner. All three of the men had gone fishing for the day, leaving Ellen behind at her own insistence. Enormously relieved that she wouldn't have to face Jonathan soon, Fran was able to face the day with something akin to anticipation, knowing that in Ellen's company she was unlikely to have the opportunity to brood.

"What would you like to do?" Fran asked a few minutes later when she returned from the kitchen, after requesting the housekeepers serve she and Ellen coffee, orange juice and toast out on the patio.

"You know what I'd really like to do?" Ellen lowered her voice conspiratorially and had the mischievous look of a child. "I'd like to do the real tourist bit, including a ride on one of those adorable little Conch Trains I saw yesterday afternoon. Bill just hates the very idea of sightseeing like a regular tourist—I think it's a point of pride with him. That's why it's so exciting that you're off work and the men are off our hands for the whole day!"

"Would you believe I've never ridden on one of those trains myself," Fran exclaimed, feeling herself caught up in Ellen's enthusiasm. "I think it would be fun!"

"You *have* been to Sunset at Mallory Square?" Ellen demanded.

Fran picked up the glass of orange juice Joanna had just set in front of her and took a big gulp, taken by surprise with the question. "Sure, lots of times."

"I had heard about it from a friend of ours, actually more of an acquaintance—but you've probably met her—Anne Taylor?" At Fran's startled nod of agreement, Ellen rushed on. "When Anne said it was boring and not to bother going if I ever got down here, I knew right then it was something I shouldn't miss! I had to twist Jonathan's arm yesterday afternoon to make him take us. He made every excuse in the book. I'm not sure it was such a good idea, either. He was in a dreadful mood by the time we left the place."

Fran was a little dazed at the rapidity of Ellen's chatter, but didn't want her to stop. "Jonathan can be moody at times," she offered.

"I just can't believe he's spending so much time down here, away from his business and the family place."

Fran could think of no reply whatever and had to content herself with what she meant to be sympathetic silence.

"He's always been so devoted to Maine. We all make fun of him and call him a 'down easter,' but it never fazes him. Then he ups and leases this place and spends all his spare time here. Everybody's been dying to know what was going on."

"You knew he has invested in several old houses and is restoring them, with Larry's help?"

"Phooey! That's no reason. Larry doesn't need Jonathan looking over his shoulder, and Jonathan knows it. No, I knew there was something drawing Jonathan to Key West, and the secret is out now." Ellen's knowing look made Fran want to squirm. Heavens, she didn't think Jonathan was coming to Key West because of *her*? But then maybe Jonathan hadn't told the Aldens the truth about his engagement to Fran.

"Did you enjoy Sunset?" Fran decided it was time to change the subject.

"I loved it! I only wish *I* had been adventurous enough to do something like that when I was young and had the opportunity."

Fran could only stare, astonished.

"Bill and Jonathan looked at me the same way when I told them that!" Ellen giggled delightedly. "No, I mean it. I think it's wonderful for young people to try out their wings and just be free for a while before they get tied down. There's time enough for college and career and family."

"Ellen." Something in Fran's tone sobered the older woman and drew her undivided attention. "Did Jonathan happen to mention anything to you about my— background?"

"Not a thing, dear, except that he met you here in Key West. I have to admit I was curious and tried to worm some information out of him. Without any success, I might add. Jonathan can be as uncommunicative as any man I've ever known—but I guess you must know that."

Impulsively Fran found herself telling Ellen of how

she had met Jonathan and what had happened since, including the truth about their so-called "engagement." Afterward she was relieved that Ellen knew the truth.

"What a fascinating story—and how romantic!" Ellen breathed thoughtfully, but surprisingly did not ask any questions or pursue the subject to any greater length. "Look at the time! We'd better get started with our sightseeing adventure."

Fran was vaguely disappointed that Ellen wasn't more responsive to the confidence, but it *was* time they got on their way. Before long she found herself sharing Ellen's unabashed enthusiasm while taking in the tourist attractions of Key West.

They took the Triumph convertible down to the Conch Train depot and purchased tickets for the next tour. Never in the past had Fran felt so relaxed in the company of someone she had known for such a short time. The two giggled constantly over silly little quips. The tour driver, a droll man full of jokes and anecdotes about the past inhabitants of Key West, added to their hilarity.

The tour lasted nearly two hours and afterward they set out to inspect at closer quarters some of the attractions they had passed. Audubon House was an old home where, according to local legend, the famous artist had once stayed as a guest. It was beautifully restored and furnished with antiques. On display was one of Audubon's famous portfolios of drawings.

Next they took a tour of Ernest Hemingway's house, a unique Spanish building with generous verandas at the lower level and a cool, encircling balcony on the second floor. Everywhere Fran looked were cats of every possible description and color, many of which had six toes on each foot and were reputed descendants of the famous author's own pets. The large rectangular

152

pool behind the house, next to the guest cottage, was the first swimming pool to be constructed in Key West, a surprise gift for Hemingway by his second wife.

Ellen, it seemed, was tireless. They visited the aquarium, the turtle kraals, the Handprinted Fabric factory, the Spanish galleon and the East Martello Gallery and Museum. Fran drove them all over the island, pointing out the various beaches, marinas, well-known restaurants and other places of interest the train tour had not included. At Ellen's request they went again to the point on the island claimed to be the southernmost projection of the continental United States, where a huge selection of shells were displayed for sale.

There she purchased a lovely Conch shell. "I found it so confusing at first," she confessed to the old man taking her money and digging into his pocket for change. "A native Key Wester is a Conch, and there's conch this and that on the menus. Everybody talks about Conch houses and Conch architecture. And the word is pronounced *konk,* such an unlikely harsh sound for something so beautiful!" She held up the fragile pink shell with its exquisite coiled shape.

Fran, who had been standing by quietly, smothered a giggle at the patient expression on the old man's seamed and deeply tanned visage. For him, listening to the ramblings of tourists was all in a day's work.

It was nearly four o'clock when they passed Garrison Bight, where most of the fishing charter boats docked. Fran recalled too late that this was about the time the boats began to return with their tired, exultant charterers. One of the big free attractions in Key West was a stroll along the docks of Garrison Bight at four o'clock to view the bustle of activity as giant fish were unloaded and hung under the name boards of the respective boats.

There was invariably a flurry of picture-taking before the hardworking mate on each boat could get down to the business of cleaning and dressing whatever fish the charterers chose to keep. Enterprising taxidermists strolled the length of the docks handing out business cards, hoping to profit from the aftermath of excitement at having caught a "big one."

"Hey, Fran, look at the people over there! What's going on?" Ellen was far too alert to miss anything, and Fran had no choice other than to explain, knowing even as she did that Ellen would want to stop. Fran's only hope was the knowledge that people with lots of money could talk the boat captains into staying out longer than the standard schedule. There was a slim chance she and Ellen might not run into Jonathan's party at the docks.

Various boats began to approach the dock, which now became thickly congested with people, some who had been out on the blue water all day fishing, others like Fran and Ellen just there to watch the activity. The air rang with greetings and good-natured exchanges between captains and mates, while prospective charterers roamed up and down eyeing the day's catches with envious appreciation.

Fran bit her lip and finally forced out the question foremost in her mind. "What's the name of the boat Bill chartered?"

"You know, I've been standing here mentally kicking myself for not asking! It just didn't seem important at the time. Why don't we just walk up and down and see if we can spot them?"

Fran saw them before Ellen did, and her heart seemed to catapult somewhere in the vicinity of her throat at the sight of Jonathan, as deeply bronzed and rugged as any of the fit young mates aboard the other boats. He and Bill were helping their bearded crewman unload a bountiful catch, while Larry stood on the dock watching, appearing vastly relieved to have the whole fishing trip over.

*"Bill!"*

Ellen's voice cut right through the hubbub, catching the attention of her husband and the tall man bent over beside him. They both looked up, surprised, and Jonathan's eyes quickly searched beyond Ellen and found Fran. For a long moment her eyes locked with his before he transferred his attention back to completing the task of unloading the fish.

Fran was shaken by that long searching gaze, which had seemed to plumb the depths of her soul. To cover her confusion, she went over to Larry and engaged him in a meaningless conversation to which she barely paid attention, all her nerves finely tuned to the moment when Jonathan would step up on the dock. Her apprehension about the encounter was needless, as it turned out. He barely acknowledged her presence when he and Bill leaped from the boat to join her and Larry and Ellen standing in front of the impressive array of fish the men had caught.

Ellen overruled all protests to the contrary and insisted the three fishermen pose, along with their captain and mate, beside their catch. "Don't let them fool you," she said in an aside to Fran. "Bill wants this picture as much as I do. Wait and see who has it enlarged and framed."

Jonathan's tall, rugged figure was like a magnet drawing Fran's gaze, and it was with the greatest difficulty that she kept herself from looking at him. To her relief, the picture-taking was finally over, and the men became busy instructing the mate about which fish they desired cleaned.

"What happens to the rest of the fish?" Ellen wanted to know.

Larry was standing close to them, detached from the flurry of activity and clearly impatient to have all the fuss over. "Jonathan says the other fish are sold in

155

the rough to a local fish market and the proceeds split between the boat owner, usually the captain himself, and the mate." He flexed his rounded shoulders tiredly. "Say, you two don't have to hang around and wait for us."

"I wouldn't miss it for the world!" Ellen exclaimed.

At that, a hopeful expression flashed across Larry's face. His eyes questioned Fran's with a hint of pleading, and she smiled her willingness, eager for her own private reasons not to stand around any longer. The transfer of passengers was arranged with Ellen, who agreed readily to accompanying Bill and Jonathan in their car, while Larry and Fran left immediately in the Triumph.

"Hope you don't mind the stench of fish and male perspiration," Larry apologized, leaning back in the passenger seat of the small car with a groan.

"Didn't you have a good time?" Fran inquired curiously. His whole attitude toward the fishing trip was less than enthusiastic.

"This is the second time in a month I've been shanghaied to go out on a boat. One of these days Jonathan is going to push the limits of our friendship too far."

Fran had turned off Roosevelt Boulevard and was driving slowly through a quiet residential section. She gave him a puzzled look. "I wondered why you didn't mention the fishing trip last night."

"I had no intention of going. Boats really aren't my thing. Especially not all day. Jonathan woke me at dawn this morning and fairly insisted I join the party." At her frown, he reached over and patted her hand on the steering wheel. "It's over and I survived, as usual. Whoops! Sorry, I didn't mean to touch you."

When the car stopped in the driveway, he didn't lose a second getting out, declaring his eagerness to shower off the fish residue and change. "Get ready for the fish stories," he flung over his shoulder, leaving her to park the car in the detached garage.

After the rigorous day of sightseeing with Ellen, Fran was a little tired herself and decided in favor of a swim before changing for dinner. She was swimming the length of the pool in smooth, rhythmic strokes when she heard a jocular voice. "Great minds!" Larry stood at the edge of the pool, his hair slicked down from his shower, wearing the loose green bathing suit which seemed to be his one and only. Fran regretted the inevitable comparison between his stocky, almost pudgy build and Jonathan's tall, muscled frame.

"Come on in! The water's fine!" she joked.

When the others arrived, she and Larry were sitting side by side on the edge of the pool, leaning back on braced arms and kicking idly at the water with their bare feet. Fran was utterly relaxed after the vigorous exercise of swimming and was enjoying the desultory conversation with Larry, who could be a droll companion when he didn't go serious on her.

"Bill, don't look!" Ellen's voice bubbled with laughter. "Fran, there must be *some* local law against looking the way you do in that teensy yellow bikini!"

"Don't move, Fran, I'll be right there!" Bill boomed, coming up behind Ellen and looping an incredibly long arm around her shoulder.

Their high spirits were infectious, and Fran's mouth curved into a smile even as she looked beyond the couple for Jonathan. He was nowhere to be seen. It took all her self-discipline not to look up toward his room, which like hers overlooked the pool.

Fifteen minutes later when Ellen and Bill returned, Jonathan was with them, but Fran was able to spare him only a glance because Bill, who without doubt had the longest, skinniest legs Fran had ever seen, wasted no time in scooping her up and dumping her unceremoniously into the pool. At the first opportunity, she retaliated by swimming beneath him when he was floating on the surface and dragging him under by a skinny ankle. The pool became a scene of much gaiety for the next hour.

All the reserve that Fran might have expected to feel around Jonathan's friends evaporated in the warm, friendly atmosphere they created by their very personalities. Only once during the evening did it occur to her to marvel that she, Fran Bright, was so totally relaxed that she might really have *belonged* in this luxurious setting.

The mood of tired casualness continued into the evening. They sat around the pool in their swimsuits, sipping before-dinner drinks prepared and served by Jonathan. Fran's was straight fruit juice. Except for a glass of wine with dinner, she still abstained from alcoholic beverages, unable to countenance the misery of another hangover like the one she'd suffered.

Finally someone stood and reluctantly announced the intention of changing for dinner. "Let's keep it simple," Bill suggested and everyone immediately agreed. It had been a long and pleasantly tiring day for all of them, and soon after the meal, yawns became more and more evident.

"I think I'd better go to bed before somebody has to carry me," Larry announced wearily and then held up his hands as if to ward off physical blows. "Okay, okay, you guys! Save your compliments!"

"I was only going to say that between us Jonathan and I might manage to get you to the foot of the stairs," Bill reproached.

It was the signal everyone needed to break up the party. Fran was about to troop after the others when Jonathan's voice stopped her.

"Fran, could I talk to you a minute?"

She stiffened in dread and turned around slowly to

meet his gaze. Tonight he hadn't paid her any special attention, and she had pushed aside the memory of the disturbing interlude by the pool last night, willing, if he was, to pretend it had never happened.

"Sit down," he ordered in a low, impatient voice. "It's not an execution."

She took the chair he indicated, sitting stiffly erect. "What did you want?"

He seemed to turn her hesitant question over in his mind, his mouth twisted in an ironic half smile. "I'm not sure I want to answer that truthfully at the moment," he answered cryptically. "I do want to ask your forgiveness for what happened last night. There isn't really any excuse to offer for my behavior except—" He shook his head dismissively as if the reason somehow wasn't worth voicing.

Fran was swamped by confusion. His apology was the last thing she expected, and she wished fervently he would have finished explaining that "excuse." His regret for what had happened between them was obvious in his tone and expression, and the reason for it was all too obvious and painful—he didn't want to foster in her a hope that their relationship could ever be permanent. And if that realization wasn't distressing enough, she remembered how he had stopped making love to her so suddenly, and wondered if a man like Jonathan could possibly be satisfied with someone as inexperienced as she. It wasn't likely.

"Well?" His husky voice interrupted her troubled introspection. "Am I forgiven?"

Torn between instinctive honesty, which required her to admit there was nothing to forgive since she had wanted him to make love to her last night, and an equally powerful urge to protect her pride, Fran said as little as possible. "Don't worry about it. It isn't important." All the while she was compellingly aware of just how important it was. The man she loved was apologizing because he had kissed and caressed her while she had responded with all the ardor of her awakened passion.

Jonathan shifted restlessly in his chair, running long fingers through his rumpled dark hair. Fran, watching the movement with intense longing, remembered how his hair had felt to her eager fingers last night, crisp and vital.

"Fran, I don't want to embarrass you, but—I really have to know. Last night for a while you seemed to respond, and I thought perhaps you might be getting over the aversion to any kind of sexual contact. Then all of a sudden, you went still in my arms, and I knew you hadn't conquered your feelings. That *is*—why you ran?"

Fran absorbed his words somewhat dazedly, having been taken yet again utterly by surprise. He thought her pulling away from him last night was the rejection of sexual intimacy she had displayed very early in their relationship, when nothing was further from the truth. She had wanted Jonathan to make love to her. At no time last night had she experienced the slightest revulsion at his touch. Unwittingly, though, he was offering her an avenue that would save her pride.

"Yes, Jonathan," she whispered. It took enormous effort to utter that lie. She wished with all her heart she could tell him the truth: her love for him had purged her psyche of the irrational guilt she had once suffered for feelings that were perfectly normal in human beings. Thanks to Jonathan, she had shaken the stranglehold of her father's bitterness toward all women.

"I promise you it won't happen again—not if I can help it." Jonathan's voice seemed to come from some place deep inside him, and it touched her with its tired resignation. His face was somber and deeply thoughtful. Fran felt as if he had already left her, and she wished despairingly that everything could have been different.

Fran watched a sleek dark head bob up next to a crimson bathing cap and experienced an all-too-familiar stab of bitterness. Had Jonathan invited Anne Taylor to Key West? The blonde woman had certainly done her best to give Fran that impression. She seemed always to be at Garrett House these days, and she and Jonathan appeared inseparable, leaving Fran paired with Larry, much to his satisfaction.

So much for the pretense of her engagement to Jonathan. She still wore the sumptuous sapphire ring, but it was the only reminder of the make-believe relationship. Ellen knew the truth and doubtlessly had shared it with her husband. Larry had known almost from the first thanks to Fran's impulsive confidence, and Anne had plainly not believed at the outset that Jonathan would tie himself down to a nobody like Fran.

Jonathan . . . Her eyes sought the dark head again, and she waited for the inevitable pain to constrict her chest. He might have been a polite stranger the last few days, judging from his distant manner with her. Sometimes she felt he didn't even know she was *there*, among the group. Not once since the night of their conversation on the patio had she found herself alone in his company. On several occasions she had looked up to find him staring at her with an expression in the gray eyes that gripped her heart with fear—it was an expression of profound regret.

Was Jonathan sorry now he had altered her life and forced her to live in his house, to associate with his friends and live by a different scale of values? Had she become an embarrassment to him, an unwanted burden, an obstacle between Anne and himself, as Anne.

repeatedly insinuated whenever she could get Fran alone?

"Fran, why are you hovering over there on the patio all by yourself, looking as if the world will come to an untimely end in just five minutes?"

Ellen's good-natured demand jerked Fran out of the paralysis induced by her somber introspection. "Actually, I'm just admiring all the beautiful suntanned bodies," she called lightly, approaching the pool. The remark, as she intended, set off an inevitable series of amiably deprecating comments and drew the attention away from herself.

"Well, if we were seriously awarding a prize for the most beautiful suntanned body in our midst," Bill's voice rose above the clamor, "I know who would get *my* vote."

Fran was hardly aware of his pointed glance at her because Jonathan and Anne had climbed out of the pool and were standing close by.

"Thank you, darling!" Ellen chirped, deliberately misinterpreting his remark, and everyone laughed appreciatively except Anne, who managed a smile marked by boredom.

"Could we please change the subject to something besides bodies?" Larry begged humorously, and then covered his head as if to protect it from a barrage of uncomplimentary remarks.

"Come on, Larry," Fran invited. "Let's swim some laps." Involuntarily her eyes went to Jonathan's. Did he miss those times when just the two of them would swim themselves to exhaustion, engaging in an unspoken competition of stamina in which he was inevitably the winner? She still swam very early in the morning before Larry was even up, but Jonathan no longer joined her.

"Fran's determined to get old Larry here in shape," Bill scoffed. "Personally I don't know why she wastes her time with *him,* when I have so much potential!" He assumed a classic bodybuilder's pose, ridiculously comic in view of the length and pronounced thinness of his limbs.

"You're all hopeless," Fran insisted, shaking her head and turning to plunge head first into the pool. Had the rest of them noticed Jonathan's silence throughout the lighthearted exchange? Had anyone else seen the way those gray eyes rested upon her with such gravity?

Later in the afternoon, when they were all sitting around sipping cool drinks, she wondered if she had imagined Jonathan's earlier restraint. He seemed perfectly relaxed in his role as host, making drinks for everyone according to their wish, adding a comment here and there to show he was keeping abreast of the conversation, which took a turn totally unexpected for Fran.

"This is the first time I've ever *not* been eager to get back home to Boston after a vacation," Ellen reflected with regret. "Fran's right—Key West does get into your bloodstream."

"You're not thinking of leaving already!" Dismay rang in Fran's spontaneous protest and shone in her clear turquoise eyes. Up until now no mention had been made about the Aldens' visit coming to an end. She liked both of them so much the thought of their leaving wrenched unpleasantly.

"Just as I feared. The beautiful lass *has* fallen for me," Bill said lugubriously, attempting to alleviate the serious mood which had suddenly descended upon the party.

"Looks like *most* of us will be leaving Key West in the next few days," Anne remarked smugly, her eyes meeting Fran's with a gleam of malicious triumph.

"Not me—not Fran," Larry retorted, his tone and expression making it clear that he would be able to

163

withstand the departure of all the others as long as Fran remained. An awkward silence followed.

"Are you finally getting back to work, Jonathan?" Ellen inquired. "I was beginning to wonder if you'd taken on the permanent role of tycoon playboy."

He frowned at her words and sounded mildly irritated when he spoke. "For your information, dear lady, I've been *back to work*, as you put it, the whole time via telephone. I am thinking of spending the better part of the summer in Maine. This tropical sun is fine, but I can't risk melting all the New England ice in my veins." His voice was light and discouraged any further question or comment concerning his plans.

Fran's heart plummeted like a lead boulder at this revelation that Jonathan intended to leave Key West. In spite of his deliberate vagueness, she sensed a finality that chilled her with fear. He had left before numerous times during the past months, but always with the understanding that he would soon return. This time was different.

Troubling questions crowded her mind. Did he plan to retain the lease on Garrett House? Was she to continue living according to the terms of her pact with him?

"Cheer up, Fran, you look like you're about to burst into tears at the prospect of our mass exodus," Ellen chided sympathetically. "You can always come up and visit us in rocky old New England."

Without warning Fran's eyes sought Jonathan's and found them fixed upon her in a brooding expression. He didn't second Ellen's invitation, and the omission flooded Fran with hopelessness. Evidently he had no desire for her to invade his real life once he had left her behind.

"I've never been farther north than Georgia," she admitted with a wistfulness that surprised her. When had the desire to see more of the world been born in her? Before she met Jonathan, she had been content never to leave Key West at all.

"Marry me, baby, and I'll take you 'round the world," Larry quipped facetiously, but the expression in his eyes as he looked at her told everyone he was perfectly serious.

"That's a very tempting offer, Larry," she said warmly, the cold detachment on Jonathan's face rankling deeply and making her determined to show him she could get along without his help.

Before the evening was over, she would have double cause to regret those words to Larry. The first instance occurred when she was dressing for dinner a short time later. She had just zipped herself into a soft white dress, one of her favorites, when she remembered that it was the same dress she had worn the evening Jonathan gave her the sapphire ring. That same evening she had agreed to the sham engagement and later sparred with Anne and gotten herself disastrously drunk.

Looking down at the exquisite ring she still wore on her left hand, she was overwhelmed anew with its beauty and obvious value. Now that Jonathan was leaving Key West, there would be no need for her to wear it any longer. She must give it back to him.

So sunk was she in the pain of her thoughts she didn't hear the door open quietly, or realize someone else was in the room, until Anne spoke in a sneering voice. "Just can't make up your mind between them, can you? Can't decide who's the better catch!"

Fran whirled, startled. "How dare you barge into my room without knocking?"

"Listen to her—'how dare you barge into *my* room'!" Anne mocked with a snide little smile and came further into the room. "You have a lot of nerve talking to me like that, as though *you* have any business living in this house at all. If Jonathan didn't have such a guilty conscience about you, you'd have been out of here weeks ago. I know because he told me exactly the way he feels."

Furious both at her manner and her words, Fran was torn between ordering her to get out of the room immediately and allowing her to continue. The latter urge won.

"Suppose *you* tell *me*," Fran suggested icily, backing up to sit on the bench of the vanity in order to conceal the uncontrollable trembling which had seized her legs.

Anne went over to perch on the edge of Fran's bed, the two of them forming a travesty of women friends engaging in a chat.

"Jonathan's hoping you'll take poor Larry up on his proposal before the fool comes to his senses and realizes how unsuited someone like you is to be the wife of a successful man. It would take care of a very embarrassing situation for Jonathan, because *I* refuse to marry him until you're out of his hair."

Fran wanted desperately not to believe a word she was saying, but what other explanation was there for Jonathan's constrained manner, the brooding regret in his eyes when he looked at Fran. For several seconds, the agony of having her deepest fears confirmed made it impossible for her to speak. She stared down at the magnificent blue gem and the diamonds sparkling on each side of it.

"Why didn't Jonathan tell me all this himself?" Fran's tightly controlled voice was a triumph of will over emotion.

Anne smiled pityingly. "Let's be honest with each other, shall we? Everyone—with the possible exception of poor Larry—knows why Jonathan picked you up off the streets. He's had his diversion—" Fran had come to her feet at those words and Anne raised a manicured hand as if to ward her off. "Let me finish, please. Now he would like to be rid of you and just doesn't want to cause a big scene around his friends. He's taking the easy way out by going back to Maine, hoping you'll finally get the idea. Personally I don't think it's fair to leave you hanging like this." She lifted her shoulders in an expressive shrug and eyed Fran speculatively with cold blue eyes, awaiting her response.

While Anne spoke, Fran had gone a gamut of emotions ranging from unbearable pain to a deep, cold anger. This last caused her voice to vibrate her scorn as she replied. "And *you*, in your sense of fair play, have come on your own to tell me that Jonathan would like to get rid of me." Her lip curled to emphasize her skepticism. "I'm having a little trouble believing the unselfishness of your motives, Anne. I suggest you let Jonathan tell me his own thoughts—or are you afraid of what they might be?"

"You little bitch!" Anne jumped to her feet, her hands clenched into fists as if she would like to physically attack Fran. "There's only one thing Jonathan ever wanted from you, and either he didn't get it or he's tired of it already. *You* know the answer to that one better than I do! If you know what's good for you, you'll marry Larry while he's still willing." She swept out of the room, slamming the door behind her.

Fran sank back down on the bench behind her, the tremulousness in her legs becoming an ague that shook her whole body. She retained enough judgment to recognize the venom in Anne's words as a cruel effort to inflict pain, but it was the truth in them that burned into her soul like redhot coals. Aside from the hurt that came from knowing Jonathan did not return her love and never would, her distress was compounded by the thought of his marrying someone as vicious and spiteful as Anne. How could he love her? Couldn't he see beyond the beautiful face and perfect figure?

She didn't know how long she sat hunched over on the bench, going over and over the words and phrases, wondering what she was going to do, when a tap on her door roused her dully to the present.

"Fran? You in there? We're all waiting dinner for you." Larry sounded vaguely anxious.

"Be right down, Larry." Could that voice, calm and normal, really be hers when she felt irreparably broken?

What was even more extraordinary was her ability during dinner to act as if nothing in the world had happened to destroy her hopes for the future, tenuous as they might have been. She managed to carry on her part of the conversation and even to produce a sound remarkably like her normal laughter.

The only time she came close to breaking was when she looked up to find Jonathan's eyes fixed bleakly on the sapphire ring on her hand. It seemed to burn her flesh, and she repressed an overwhelming urge to wrench it off and hand it to him then and there. What must he be thinking to have the bone structure of his face hardened into stone and his eyes opaque like pebbles of granite? Did he think she wore the ring to remind him of his obligations to her?

At the next opportunity she would give the ring back to him. No, she decided with sudden fierce resolution, she'd return it that very night, even if she had to wait until everyone went to bed and take it to him in his room.

# Chapter Ten

Larry had been even more attentive and possessive than usual, giving Fran additional cause to regret those words spoken so impulsively that afternoon. Still, when he suggested a walk, she agreed, finding Anne's knowing smiles more than she could tolerate.

They hadn't walked very far before Larry reached for her hand. "Were you only joking this afternoon when you intimated you might consider marrying me?" he asked hopefully.

Fran felt like a criminal for having falsely raised his hopes in the attempt to irritate Jonathan for his indifference. "Larry, I don't love you," she said in a low, apologetic voice, stopping on the sidewalk and facing him squarely. He was dear and solid and it would have been far better for her to fall in love with him than with Jonathan, but she hadn't. The kindest thing was to make her feelings clear.

"What if I'm willing to take the chance you will learn

to care for me. There isn't anyone else, is there?" He studied her downcast head.

Slowly she lifted her face so that he could read the admission there. It was written in the misery of her clear eyes, the droop of her full, sensitive mouth.

"Jonathan?"

"Yes. Jonathan," she said, her voice breaking on the name.

"That jerk," he muttered, and then groaned. "What am I saying? Don't pay any attention to me—you know he's my best friend in the world. I'm just jealous as hell." He draped an arm around her shoulders and slowly they began walking again, wrapped in their common knowledge.

"Does he know?"

She shook her head, still full of self-reproach that she was hurting Larry just as Jonathan was hurting her, but she was too fond of Larry not to tell him the truth. Her own heartache made her more sensitive than usual to the disappointment of a fellow human, especially one as fine and generous as Larry.

"What do you plan to do?" he prodded gently but insistently.

"I don't know what to do. I can't impose on Jonathan any longer, not after tonight." She told him about the scene with Anne in her bedroom.

He was silent, mulling over the account she had given. "Sounds like wishful thinking on her part. Anne's been after Jonathan since the beginning of time. I admit I'm pretty amazed at the attention he's been paying her lately. But I still find it hard to believe—"

For Fran, the subject was too painful to continue. "I guess I'll have to find myself a place to live. Maybe Eleanor will keep me on at the shop anyway. If she does, I'll be able to go to school part-time." She hesitated. "I know what I'd *like* to study."

"What?" He was arrested by the diffidence in her voice.

"Architecture. Don't laugh at me—I know I'm probably not smart enough." She didn't look at him for fear of what she might read on the honest face.

"I'm not laughing. In fact, I'm very flattered, and I've no doubt whatever you're smart enough."

They soon turned around and went back to the house. The others had evidently gone out without them, and Fran watched television with Larry for a short time before going to her room. Much of her fatigue was due to the emotional rigors of the past twelve hours.

She had drifted off into a light sleep when she was awakened by voices: Ellen's high-pitched tone and the lower masculine cadences of Jonathan and Bill. They were back. Almost instantly she dozed again, only dimly aware of doors opening and closing.

Then suddenly she awoke, disturbed by a sense of urgency that there was something she must do—now, tonight. The ring. She had to return the ring to Jonathan. Under the present circumstances she couldn't bear to keep it another hour and have him think badly of her.

Singleminded in her determination, she climbed out of bed and headed for the door, her mind too clouded with sleep to dictate the propriety of a robe to cover her nightgown. There was no immediate response to her tentative tap on Jonathan's door. She waited a few moments, and then knocked again. This time the door swung open and Jonathan stood there, naked to the waist, staring incredulously at her.

Twisting the ring off her finger, she whispered, "I wanted to give this back to you. I can't keep it now."

His expression was savage as he lifted one arm and propped himself against the door facing, his eyes raking her figure in the semitransparence of the dainty nylon and lace gown. For the first time, she became aware of its inadequacy in concealing her figure.

"I suppose Larry objects to your possessing a ring given to you by another man." The effort to keep his voice low only intensified the tone of controlled violence.

With a lightning movement he straightened and turned away from her, walking several steps toward the center of the room, where he stood with his back to her. Automatically, she followed him, momentarily so strongly conscious of him, the breadth and power of the wide shoulders, the taut muscles of his back, the tapering slimness of his waist, that she forgot why she had come. In her present state of being half asleep, his virility was having a noticeable impact.

Then she looked down and saw the ring she held in the palm of her hand and remembered her purpose. "Larry has nothing to do with it. I just can't keep anything this valuable." When he didn't speak, she took a few tentative steps toward his bureau. "I'll just put it over here."

He pivoted abruptly, taking her so by surprise that she jumped and stared at him, frightened. "Get out of here, Fran, and take that ring with you! Now!"

She was strangely frozen, puzzled by his hostility at her efforts to return the ring, and at the same time captivated by the potency of his masculinity. Her eyes were intrigued by his smooth brown skin and underlying muscles tensed now with his incomprehensible anger. He stood with legs braced apart, the dark material of his trousers molding the hard sinews of his thighs.

"I'm sorry, Jonathan," she finally managed to murmur, wishing she could do or say something to appease him, to bring back the warm companion of the past.

His eyes darkened with some unfathomable emotion as he took a half step toward her and then checked himself, wheeling around with a low groan. "Why, in the name of heaven, should *you* be sorry," he asked in a tormented voice. "If anyone should be sorry, I'm the one."

Those words confirmed her deepest fears. Anne had been right. Jonathan wished now he had never interfered in her life—he didn't even want to look at her. Deprived of all hope, Fran padded quietly to the bureau, laid the ring down on the polished surface, and left his room.

The final days of vacation for Ellen and Bill passed all too quickly for Fran, who managed, she thought, to do a creditable job of concealing her aching unhappiness. She would miss them when they were gone.

The day of their departure came, and with it the reminder that Jonathan, too, would soon be leaving, returning to his beloved Maine for an unstated period of time. Somehow Fran didn't think he would ever come back to Key West.

Her emotions got the better of her when the time came for Bill and Ellen to go to the airport to catch their plane. In spite of valiant efforts toward self-control, Fran felt the tears well and spill down her cheeks when she hugged Ellen goodbye. The other woman's eyes were suspiciously bright as she scolded, "I hate these goodbye scenes. Bill and I were honestly tempted to pack our bags and sneak out early this morning before any of you were awake."

The men were stowing the luggage in the trunk of Jonathan's car, giving Ellen an opportunity for a private word with Fran. "Thank you again for everything. And don't worry, honey. As long as you're here, Jonathan won't be able to stay away from Key West, in spite of his brave words about spending the summer in Maine."

She gave Fran another quick hug and called over her

shoulder, "Okay, okay, you guys, I'm coming!" She climbed into the front seat to sit between Jonathan and Bill and waved to Fran and Larry, who stood beside the driveway together, watching the car pull out onto the street and then accelerate out of sight.

"They're so nice," Fran said softly, her mind grappling with Ellen's parting comments. She obviously still held to her belief that Fran was Jonathan's reason for having spent so much time in Key West during the past months. Fran wished that Ellen's mistaken perceptions were true, but they weren't.

"Say, how about going out with me tonight?" Larry invited, his eyes taking in the downcast features.

Why not? she thought wearily. Jonathan no doubt would be busy with Anne now that he no longer had house guests to entertain. "I'd like that, Larry," she accepted, trying to inject a little enthusiasm into her voice and to muster a smile.

Some hours later she was finished dressing and about to leave her room to go downstairs to meet Larry when there was a staccato knock on her door. She knew it was Jonathan.

"Come in," she bade in a voice that was choked by the sudden constriction in her throat.

The door swung open and Jonathan stood there staring at her with gray eyes that gave no hint of his thoughts. "Larry informs me you're going out together tonight."

"That's right," she said, intensely conscious of him, tall and stern and forbidding, and yet overpoweringly masculine. Every time she looked at him now it was with the realization that he soon would be gone.

"In that case, I might as well say goodbye now. I'll be leaving before daylight and probably won't have another opportunity."

"But why didn't you tell me earlier?" she protested.

"I wouldn't have agreed to go out your last night here. Larry won't mind if we change our plans and stay—"

"Don't bother," he interrupted curtly. "Actually I've plans to dine out myself."

Humiliation and hurt washed through her as she realized he didn't wish to be bothered with her company that evening, his last evening in Key West. She could guess who his dinner companion was—Anne.

"I just wanted to reassure you that my absence doesn't change anything for you. I shall continue to lease this house—"

"That won't be necessary!" she interrupted, stung to the quick by the cold indifference in his voice and face. She couldn't bear to let him finish that rehearsed little speech without informing him that she wanted nothing more from him.

"How foolish of me!" he mocked before she could even explain that she intended to move out and rent a place of her own. "I forget that you and Larry will probably want a place of your own. Just in case I'm not around for the wedding—which might be a little more than I could stomach—why don't I kiss the prospective bride now?"

Mesmerized by the wild glitter in the gray eyes, she stood dumb while he crossed the space between them in two long strides and pulled her against him without any gentleness. His mouth ground against hers in a brutal, punishing kiss that contained no element of affection or consideration, only anger and violence. The rough aggression of his hands and lips imparted insult and humiliation, but Fran submitted to them without any effort to break away. Nothing could change the fact that she loved him, and her hands would have crept up around his neck if they hadn't been trapped against the hard wall of his chest.

The assault ended as precipitously as it began, Jonathan wrenching himself away from her with a curse, throwing her off balance, and then striding out of the room without a further word.

She was quite shaken by the tormented violence in his countenance and in his treatment of her. Jonathan seemed to hate her, and she couldn't think of any reason that should be so. What had happened, what had she done to arouse that kind of dark emotion? It was unendurable to have their last meeting end like this.

Fran moved through the rest of the evening like one anesthetized. She went through the motions of normality, talking, eating, even laughing, with one purpose in mind: to gain the sanctuary of her room where she would wait, in a strange state of suspension, until she knew that Jonathan was gone. Only then would she be able to collapse, as she knew she would, and submit to her loss.

She heard the car when he arrived home, and some time later the opening and closing of his bedroom door. She gave a little sigh of relief. A breeze swept through the open windows of her room, billowing the filmy curtains and wafting inside the sweet odor of frangipani from the outside darkness.

A restlessness stirred Fran and she got out of bed, feeling suddenly that she couldn't bear to be inside the walls a moment longer. The tropical evening beckoned her to come outside and maintain her strange vigil in the hushed fragrance of the patio.

Without stopping to pull on a robe, she left her room with the utmost quiet and crept down the stairs barefoot. The house was silent, and she was alone, the only person awake in the entire world. Outside she perched on the raised side of the fountain basin, absorbing the cool fragrance of the night and the silvery ripple of the water dropping from the cupped hands of the marble nymph.

There was no sound to alert her to the presence of another person, but some prickling awareness told her she was not alone. She looked around and saw Jonathan standing a few yards away, his hands thrust into the pockets of his dark robe.

"I thought you would be sleeping," she said foolishly.

"Sleep has been an unknown luxury of late," he said cryptically. "Why aren't you asleep? Too excited about marrying Larry?"

The atmosphere between them crackled with tension, but Fran noted with relief the absence of that terrible anger which had so disturbed her earlier. Suddenly she was glad of this opportunity to talk to Jonathan. She wanted to tell him how grateful she was that he had uprooted her from a pointless existence and given her a much larger perspective. While she had lost her former youthful irresponsibility and the peace of mind which had been based mostly on ignorance and laziness, in their place she had gained the beginnings of maturity and the ambition to make something of her life. Now she would have the chance to express all these feelings to him before he left, because she probably wouldn't see him again.

"Jonathan, I don't know what made you think I'm going to marry Larry," she said, "because I'm not." In her urgency, she stood and took a step toward him, completely unaware of the diaphanous sheerness of her nightgown against the subdued lighting of a lamp in the shrubbery behind her.

He turned around abruptly, and she pleaded, "Please don't go, Jonathan, I want to talk to you."

"Fran, I don't know what you expect out of me—if you know what's good for you, you'd better get back in your room!"

The harshness in his voice hurt unbearably, and the control she'd been maintaining for hours crumpled.

Sobs convulsed her slender body, but she tried desperately not to make a sound so he wouldn't see how devastated she was.

A muffled whisper must have reached his ears because he swore violently and before she could guess his intention, he had moved swiftly and taken her into his arms, crushing her hard against him and imploring in a low anguished voice, "Please don't do that, my darling." And then when her emotional storm didn't subside, "Can you ever forgive me, darling?"

From the wonderfully broad and secure warmth of his chest, Fran registered his words somewhat dazedly. "Wh-what?"

"I know I had no right to barge in and try to change you the way I did. It was damnably selfish, but I wanted to make you see how much more life has to offer—"

His voice broke off and she looked up into his face, shocked at the tormented guilt she saw there. "I don't understand—"

"You knew I saw you that afternoon at Sunset, the day Ellen and Bill arrived. You were crying your heart out, looking at that young couple and seeing what you'd given up. I realized then how wrong I'd been to tamper with the life of another human being, as though I were some kind of god, just because—" He drew her even closer, making her breathing difficult.

It was what he hadn't said that made Fran's heart pound with a wild hope. "Jonathan, why *did* you tamper with me?" she asked softly.

He buried his face into her tumbled hair so that she could barely understand the muffled words. "I couldn't help myself. The first time I saw you, I was utterly enchanted, bewitched. I had to have you for my own. But the vast differences between your world and mine seemed insurmountable. Then I conceived the idea to make you a part of my world—forgive me, I know now how wrong I was. But I can't bear to give you up, not even to Larry—"

Fran felt incredible happiness bubble up inside her. Jonathan loved her! How was it possible! She laughed against the hairy warmth of his bare chest. "Oh, Jonathan, I'm so glad you found me when you did."

His hold loosened slightly and he looked down intently at her. "You mean that, Fran? You don't despise me?"

"Despise you, Jonathan? I love you so much I—"

That was as far as she got because he smothered the rest of the words in a kiss of such urgency and long duration that she finally was forced to tear her face away in order to take in a gulp of air.

"Why didn't you tell me?"

With that demand, he scooped her up and carried her over to a chair, where once seated he cradled her close against him as though she were something very precious and breakable. "Do you realize that five minutes ago I was the most miserable man alive and now I'm the happiest?" He bent his head to take her lips again in that passionate hunger that aroused in her the aching need to press closer, to become one with his muscles and skin and bones.

His heart was pounding crazily against hers when he pulled his mouth away from hers and looked down at her with all his love in his eyes. "Now answer my question. Why didn't you tell me?"

Unhesitatingly, she told him. He listened, exclaiming abruptly, but not otherwise interrupting as she told what she overheard the night of Eleanor's party. As clearly as she could, she expressed for him the circumstances which had led her to conceal her love from him, ending with the conversation with Anne several nights ago.

"If only I'd known what was going on in that

beautiful head of yours," Jonathan said when she had finished. "The 'silly little fool' you overheard me talking about was Anne, not you. I had every hope when I talked you into that engagement that it would turn into a real one. I wanted to get my ring on your finger and mark you as mine, especially when I saw how Larry was falling head over heels."

Fran had had enough of conversation for the time being and slid her hand behind his head to draw his lips down to hers. He took little quick tastes of her mouth which stirred her to greater appetite. She sensed that he was holding back deliberately, keeping his passion under firm leash, and she understood why when he pulled away from her and smiled down with rueful tenderness.

"Darling, I want you the way a man wants the woman he loves, but as long as I know you're mine, I can wait. Maybe a psychiatrist can help you overcome the aversion you have to sex."

Fran smiled a secret smile, sitting up so that she could nuzzle her lips seductively against his. "Maybe you can wait," she murmured, "but I'm not sure *I* can."

His head jerked back and he looked searchingly at her. "You don't mean—"

"I *mean*," she mocked lovingly, her heart quickening with both the anticipation and the natural apprehension any woman feels when she is soon to make love for the first time.

"If you'd rather wait until we're married," he said in a voice still low with restraint.

Fran could see a magnification of the need she felt in his eyes and in the tightly controlled features, and she knew a sense of awe and humility as she realized how long Jonathan had wanted her, even before she comprehended the meaning of passion.

"I belong to you, Jonathan," she said simply and tightened her arms around his neck.

His eyes locked with hers in a long exchange that expressed more than words could ever convey. He stood and held her tightly against him as they entered the house. She knew no fear as he carried her up the stairs and into his bedroom, where he laid her gently across the bed.

There was still one final moment of hesitation as he bent over her, his face mirroring the intense effort to hold back the overpowering rush of his passion.

"Fran, are you sure?"

She smiled up at him, loving him for his consideration. "Jonathan, you asked me once if I trusted you. The answer is still yes." And she reached up and drew him down to her.

# Chapter Eleven

"Jonathan, is that a letter from Aunt Liz?"

Fran swung herself up on the side of the pool, eyeing the distinctive peach color of the stationery Jonathan was perusing as he sprawled back in a lounge chair nearby.

"It is," he said, looking up and holding out a hand. She got up and walked the few steps, thrilling to the warm possession in his eyes and yet still puzzling over why he would be receiving a letter from her aunt, whom he had met just once some time ago, and then through a business situation. It must have something to do with *me*, Fran thought.

Placing her hand in Jonathan's, she allowed him to pull her down on his lap. His arms closed around her, drawing her against his bare chest fragrant with his maleness. Memories of their lovemaking last night, and then again this morning, melted her against him, and she lifted her face invitingly to his.

Some time passed before Jonathan lightened the kiss

and then removed his lips a fraction away from hers to ask, "Don't you want to know what your Aunt Liz has to say?"

"Hm-m-m." Fran sat up a little trying to clear her love-drugged brain. "Why *is* Aunt Liz writing to *you*? She doesn't even know you."

"That's where you're wrong, my love," he contradicted. "Your aunt is one of my dearest friends, for always, as well as my accomplice." He laughed and Fran could hear the deep vibration in his chest.

"Your accomplice?" Even as she questioned, the surprise and curiosity were immediately tempered with the realization that she was about to learn the key to the mystery of her aunt's attitude these last months.

"Do you remember there was an interim of roughly three weeks between the time I took you to Sunset and then to dinner at the A&B Lobster House and the next time I saw you, which was the night I rescued you from your burly manager at the Black Pig?"

"Yes—"

"I left Key West the next morning after our dinner date, determined to put you completely out of my mind. Not quite three weeks later, I made a stop in Georgia on my way back here and talked to your aunt. I told her then my plans in regard to you and enlisted her aid. I've been in contact with her frequently since then."

Fran regarded him unbelievingly.

"You mean—even before you got to Key West and found out I was singing at the Black Pig and hating it and hadn't found a permanent place to live, you told Aunt Liz you planned to make a bargain with me—the other tenants could stay in the houses you owned if I moved into the house you were leasing?"

"I told her I planned to marry you, but I wasn't sure yet how to approach the matter of winning you," he corrected gently.

"Jonathan—" Fran searched his features and saw he was not teasing. "I was puzzled that Aunt Liz didn't make a bigger fuss about my living in your house. It turns out *she* trusted you, just like I did." She lifted a hand to stroke the firm line of his jaw, and the caress initiated an interlude which left both of them breathless.

"You make it very difficult to report the contents of a letter," he murmured against her neck, his lips following an irresistible route down to the cleft between her breasts, which curved tantalizingly out of the brief cups of the bikini top.

"I'm listening," she said absently, running her hands along the firm muscles of his upper arms and shoulders.

"Enough, you temptress," he said with mock severity, capturing her hands and holding them. "At my request, your aunt has done some detective work for me. I told her the little bit you revealed about your mother. At first, Liz could add nothing to it because she and her husband had already moved to Key West when your parents married, and your father and his brother apparently were not close."

Fran was alert now, with a strange feeling of expectation and dread. She yearned with all her heart to hear what Jonathan was going to tell her and yet was oddly unwilling to have him continue.

"Was Aunt Liz able to find out anything about my mother?" She moistened her dry lips with a nervous movement of her tongue.

"Yes. Do you want to hear it? You don't have to, you know."

She thought she might cry then when he said that. With characteristic sensitivity for her feelings, Jonathan sensed her deep ambivalence. She loved him even more for giving her the choice.

"It doesn't matter what the truth is. I'll still love her."

He smiled, his hand tracing the soft curve of her jawline, the fullness of her lips which quivered a little at his touch, and then the straight bridge of her nose. "As well you should. Your defensive instincts were right all along. Your mother left your father to go to relatives in Atlanta, fully intending to take legal measures to gain custody of you. She was ill at the time, or she might have tried to take you with her when she ran away. Unfortunately, she caught a flu virus, and with the infection already in her body, she wasn't able to fight it off."

Fran was silent for long moments, saddened by thoughts of the young woman who had borne her only to die without ever having lived a full, happy life. Finally, she sighed. "Thank you, Jonathan, for finding out and telling me. I always wanted to know. Somehow it isn't even important now. I don't even hate my father anymore. I think more than anything else I feel sorry for him that he missed so much."

Jonathan seemed relieved at her words, and she realized he had been quietly awaiting her reaction, perhaps experiencing some fears of his own as to the hold on her the past might still have. To reassure him completely, she said, "I'd like to visit Aunt Liz some time. I really do miss her."

He understood immediately what she was telling him: the past, with all its failures, disappointments and unhappiness, could not cast a shadow on the promise of the future at the side of this vital man who had endeared himself to her not just for his strength but perhaps even more for his gentleness.

"We can stop off and see her this afternoon if you wish. In the meantime, there's a lot to be done, such as deciding where you want to get married."

"What do you mean we could 'stop off this afternoon'?" she interrupted him.

"I have flight reservations. I thought you might like

to get married in Boston—we could call Ellen and have her arrange something simple. A friend of mine there is a judge and could perform the ceremony. Then we could go on to my place in Maine—I hope you're going to like Maine—what's wrong?" He looked up, puzzled and instantly alert, as she climbed off his lap and stood beside the chair.

"Nothing's *wrong*," she exclaimed impatiently, "except that I'm so excited I can't sit here a minute longer! We'd better get packed!"

His face eased into the smile she loved and he rose quickly with controlled power. Allowing himself one deep, passionate kiss that left her weak and clinging to him for support, he slipped an arm around her waist and walked with her toward the house.

# Genuine Silhouette sterling silver bookmark for only $15.95!

What a beautiful way to hold your place in your current romance! This genuine sterling silver bookmark, with the distinctive Silhouette symbol in elegant black, measures 1½″ long and 1″ wide. It makes a beautiful gift for yourself, and for every romantic you know! And, at only $15.95 each, including all postage and handling charges, you'll want to order several now, while supplies last.

Send your name and address with check or money order for $15.95 per bookmark ordered to

**Simon & Schuster Enterprises**
**120 Brighton Rd., P.O. Box 5020**
**Clifton, N.J. 07012**
**Attn: Bookmark**

Bookmarks can be ordered pre-paid only. No charges will be accepted. Please allow 4-6 weeks for delivery.

N.Y. State Residents
Please Add Sales Tax

# Silhouette Romance

## IT'S YOUR OWN SPECIAL TIME

*Contemporary romances for today's women.*
*Each month, six very special love stories will be yours*
*from SILHOUETTE. Look for them wherever books are sold*
*or order now from the coupon below.*

## $1.50 each

| Hampson | ☐ 1 ☐ 4 ☐ 16 ☐ 27 ☐ 28 ☐ 52 ☐ 94 | Browning | ☐ 12 ☐ 38 ☐ 53 ☐ 73 ☐ 93 |
|---|---|---|---|
| Stanford | ☐ 6 ☐ 25 ☐ 35 ☐ 46 ☐ 58 ☐ 88 | Michaels | ☐ 15 ☐ 32 ☐ 61 ☐ 87 |
| | | John | ☐ 17 ☐ 34 ☐ 57 ☐ 85 |
| Hastings | ☐ 13 ☐ 26 | Beckman | ☐ 8 ☐ 37 ☐ 54 ☐ 96 |
| Vitek | ☐ 33 ☐ 47 ☐ 84 | Wisdom | ☐ 49 ☐ 95 |
| Wildman | ☐ 29 ☐ 48 | Halston | ☐ 62 ☐ 83 |

| | | | |
|---|---|---|---|
| ☐ 5 Goforth | ☐ 22 Stephens | ☐ 50 Scott | ☐ 81 Roberts |
| ☐ 7 Lewis | ☐ 23 Edwards | ☐ 55 Ladame | ☐ 82 Dailey |
| ☐ 9 Wilson | ☐ 24 Healy | ☐ 56 Trent | ☐ 86 Adams |
| ☐ 10 Caine | ☐ 30 Dixon | ☐ 59 Vernon | ☐ 89 James |
| ☐ 11 Vernon | ☐ 31 Halldorson | ☐ 60 Hill | ☐ 90 Major |
| ☐ 14 Oliver | ☐ 36 McKay | ☐ 63 Brent | ☐ 92 McKay |
| ☐ 19 Thornton | ☐ 39 Sinclair | ☐ 71 Ripy | ☐ 97 Clay |
| ☐ 20 Fulford | ☐ 43 Robb | ☐ 76 Hardy | ☐ 98 St. George |
| ☐ 21 Richards | ☐ 45 Carroll | ☐ 78 Oliver | ☐ 99 Camp |

## $1.75 each

| Stanford | ☐ 100 ☐ 112 ☐ 131 | Browning | ☐ 113 ☐ 142 ☐ 164 ☐ 172 ☐ 191 |
|---|---|---|---|
| Hardy | ☐ 101 ☐ 130 ☐ 184 | Michaels | ☐ 114 ☐ 146 |
| Cork | ☐ 103 ☐ 148 ☐ 188 | Beckman | ☐ 124 ☐ 154 ☐ 179 |
| Vitek | ☐ 104 ☐ 139 ☐ 157 ☐ 176 | Roberts | ☐ 127 ☐ 143 ☐ 163 ☐ 180 ☐ 199 |
| Dailey | ☐ 106 ☐ 118 ☐ 153 ☐ 177 ☐ 195 | Trent | ☐ 110 ☐ 161 ☐ 193 |
| | | Wisdom | ☐ 132 ☐ 166 |
| Bright | ☐ 107 ☐ 125 | Hunter | ☐ 137 ☐ 167 ☐ 198 |
| Hampson | ☐ 108 ☐ 119 ☐ 128 ☐ 136 ☐ 147 ☐ 151 ☐ 155 ☐ 160 ☐ 178 ☐ 185 ☐ 190 ☐ 196 | Scott | ☐ 117 ☐ 169 ☐ 187 |
| | | Sinclair | ☐ 123 ☐ 174 |
| | | John | ☐ 115 ☐ 192 |

### Love So Rare by Anne Hampson

Dawn had unwillingly married Ralf Deverell, yet as the weeks passed, she realized she had fallen in love—with a husband who wanted to keep their marriage a secret.

### Her Mother's Keeper by Nora Roberts

How could anyone fall for the unscrupulous author Luke Powers? Gwen knew that she should persuade him to return to California, only now, he'd be taking her heart with him!

### Love's Sweet Music by Jean Saunders

Accompanying pianist Paul Blake on his Continental tour was a dream come true for Angela Raines. Her only fear: he saw her as another easy conquest.

### Blue Mist Of Morning by Donna Vitek

Anne Fairchild made it a rule never to get involved with her boss. However, Ty Manning left her little choice and before she knew it, he was commanding her love.

### Fountains Of Paradise by Elizabeth Hunter

Jewelry designer Michal Brent went to Sri Lanka to buy unusual and beautiful stones. But the most precious jewel she found was the jade green glance of Hendrik Van de Aa.

### Island Spell by Dorothy Cork

Working for author Guy Desailley on his island retreat was no easy task for Aidan Elliot. The attraction was immediate—but could love blossom when they were both so cynical about romance?

# READERS' COMMENTS ON SILHOUETTE ROMANCES:

"I would like to congratulate you on the most wonderful books I've had the pleasure of reading. They are a tremendous joy to those of us who have yet to meet the man of our dreams. From reading your books I quite truly believe that he will some-day appear before me like a prince!"

—L.L.*, Hollandale, MS

"Your books are great, wholesome fiction, always with an upbeat, happy ending. Thank you."

—M.D., Massena, NY

"My boyfriend always teases me about Silhouette Books. He asks me, how's my love life and natu-rally I say terrific, but I tell him that there is always room for a little more romance from Sil-houette."

—F.N., Ontario, Canada

"I would like to sincerely express my gratitude to you and your staff for bringing the pleasure of your publications to my attention. Your books are well written, mature and very contemporary."

—D.D., Staten Island, NY

*names available on request